To Judy
A magical
mystery tour through
the south.
Hope you enjoy!

CONSTELLATIONS

TIM BRYANT

Tim Bryant

Also by Tim Bryant:
Dutch Curridge
Southern Select
Spirit Trap
Keachi

CONSTELLATIONS
Tim Bryant
Copyright © 2015 Behooven Press
behoovenpress.com
twitter.com/behoovenpress

Edited by the Behooven Press Round Table.

ISBN: 978-0692430279

For Jimmy

Special thanks to the many good people
from the Nacogdoches community and
beyond who brought me firsthand knowledge
and stories of its colorful past and characters.
Each of you can be found
within these pages.

*"What show of soul are we
gonna get from you?"*

Mike Scott, The Waterboys

1: *PATTONIA*

Artillery Conray Patton stepped out of the Angelina River in the summer of 1958, ending a journey that began some forty years earlier. Several people saw him on that hot July morning, including Bill Chandler, the game warden, who was checking his trot lines before starting his daily rounds. Bill said Art surfaced from the deepest part of the channel, and he broke the surface gasping like he was wakening from a dream.

Art had nothing but the clothes on his back and a small pine box that he carried under his arm. Bill said the way he was clutching it, the way it was shaped, he thought it might hold a gun. He pushed himself into the shallows and then marched ashore, never looking once at Bill who stood right in the clear, just about where the old boat dock had once been. One end of his trot line tied off on one of three wooden beams that remained. He said Art came ashore not ten feet from him, set the box down at his feet and crumpled next to it.

"I thought he was dead for sure," Bill said. "He had a long coat on and a hat, and I really couldn't see anything but a heap of clothes and that box."

Bill approached the man, moving around him in a wide arc and then cautiously advanced.

"Don't touch the box."

Bill jumped back, startled more than afraid. He reached across and under his coat and adjusted the .38 Special in its holster. He had never drawn it on a human before, but he'd gone over scenarios for years. He felt the day coming, and he wondered if this was it.

"What's your name, boy?"

Art rolled over on his left side and pulled the hat from his head. Water seemed to pour out of him. He wiped his face with his coat sleeve and looked up. The man looked young. Certainly too young to be calling Art a boy. But that was nothing new. He also looked vaguely important.

"My name is Art."

Bill placed his hand on the revolver. It gave him a feeling of being in control.

"Whereabouts you from?" he said.

It was a standard line, usually to be followed by the

one that he'd best just get back to wherever that might be real quick. Art sat up on his left hand and waved his right from one side to the other.

"Right here. Pattonia."

Bill had been game warden in Nacogdoches County for almost ten years. He knew everybody in the area. White folks and negroes too.

"Who you belong to?"

He went down the list of negroes in the Patton's Landing area real quick. There were only three families left, and they all lived closer to Marion's Ferry. Something wasn't right. Bill pulled the gun from its holster and pointed it right at the man's head.

"I used to belong to the J.T. Conray family," Art said. "Then I became a free man."

He reached for the box and pulled it to him. It was all he had left, and if he was fated to die within sight of his old home place, it would feel better if he died holding on to something. He closed his eyes and imagined himself being pulled back under the water. He listened to the water moving away, and he thought he heard the sound of dogs barking somewhere in the rush. The sound of someone hollering.

"If I gotta go back on that damned farm again, you just as soon shoot me right here, kick my ass back in the river."

He fell into the red mud and waited. It seemed like he waited for a real long time.

2: DROP HIM AT THE BACK DOOR

When Art came ashore at Pattonia, he was wearing an undershirt, a white work shirt and black trousers. Black boots. A vest with all of the buttons missing. A long trench coat like Bill hadn't seen in years. And a hat.

Bill Chandler and a friend of his called Roy Clowney managed to get Art up the bank and to Bill's '56 Cameo pickup. He was water-logged, which doubled his weight, but his legs worked, as long as Bill and Roy were able to hold him in an upright position. The hat came off twice, at which point it was left behind, but Art never loosed his grip on the box. With him safely deposited in the truck's bed, Roy looked at Bill.

"Where you taking him?"

Bill hadn't had time to consider it.

"Should we get him to the hospital?"

Nacogdoches was a good twenty minutes away, but there wasn't anything closer.

"Will they take niggers?" Roy said.

During that day, negroes weren't welcome in most of the local restaurants. They could knock at the back door and place an order sometimes. Stores would usually let them come in the front door, as long as they had money to spend.

"Sure," said Bill, "long as we drop him at the back door."

Driving down Patton's Landing Road, they soon thought better of it. More specifically, he thought of Ivory and Oda Whitaker. Bill remembered taking a negro to their house several years earlier. He had been out in the bottoms between Nacogdoches and Lufkin and found the guy sitting against a tree and bleeding like a stuck pig.

"Somebody shoot you, boy?"

"No sir," he had said. "I fell from out this tree, trying to get at a squirrel."

Bill remembered telling the guy that he was supposed to shoot the damn things out of the tree, not climb up after them.

"What's so funny?" said Roy.

Bill turned and looked at the man in the back of his truck. He looked to be asleep, or maybe dead, but he was still holding on to that box.

5

"Think we should check out that case he's carrying?"

The only other time Bill had carried a negro in his truck— and it had been his old International that time— he had carried that squirrel hunter back toward Nacogdoches and through Marion's Ferry and dropped him off with Oda Whitaker, who was a nurse and promised to get him all fixed up and sent back home.

Bill pulled off the gravel road and onto the short pathway that led to the Whitaker place. He had no idea if the Whitakers still stayed there. Hell, who knew if they were still alive. The old house had a new coat of green paint, but the yellow still poked through here and there. Otherwise, it all looked pretty much the same. He pulled up under the same oak tree he had parked beneath before and looked at Roy.

"Old lady here's a nurse of some kind."

Roy nodded.

"I suspect we might ought check that box out," he said.

A lanky negro boy in shorts and no shirt stepped out onto the porch and then hollered out for Big Momma. Oda Whitaker suddenly appeared at the screen door. She looked irritated. Bill waved at her like they were old friends. She didn't look to be a day older.

3: THE MUSIC STICK

What was in the pine box wasn't a gun. Bill Chandler wasn't exactly sure what it was. He and Roy had both stood there eying it until Oda Whitaker came out onto the porch and down into the yard. Nothing had been said about it until the Cameo was a good half mile back down the road into Marion's Ferry.

"That was some kind of guitar," Bill said.

Roy was inspecting a field of new pines that had just been set out. Bill cranked his window down and lit a cigarette.

"Looked more like a banjer or something," Roy said. "I kind of wanted to pick on it a little."

Roy had played guitar in a western band for half of

his life, before finally settling down with a woman named Fern who followed him from town to town, bar to bar, until he finally bought her a drink, and then another drink and, before too long, a wedding ring. Now he never played or maybe he just picked now and again for Fern.

"He seemed pretty attached to it," Bill said.

It looked more like a banjo because that's what it was. A four-string gourd banjo, made out of a calabash, cut in half, a goat skin stretched across it, dried and nailed into place. The neck was made out of oak, cut from a tree that had been struck by lightning and burned to a dark almost black color, and strung with gut strings. It had been painted and repainted more than a couple of times. You could see faded designs beneath brighter colors. They seemed to tell stories in some archaic language that no one remembered. Then there were the place names and dates, each added in a different hand, a different style.

The banjo had been made in New Orleans in 1814, the year before the Battle of New Orleans. You could plainly see the city and the date etched into the gourd right where the neck was attached. After being played there for twenty years or so, it traveled upriver to Natchez (up the fretboard on the banjo) and then to Vicksburg in the 1840 before traveling to Galveston Bay and then up the Angelina River to Patton's Landing on the steamboat Laura sometime around 1860. From there, the list of colorful names wrapped back around the back of the neck and then circled the gourd. Havana. Haiti. Trinidad. Cape Verde. Dakar. Morocco. Nassau. And then back to the beginning: New Orleans.

Art Conray Patton claimed to have first seen the instrument on the cotton farm of J.T. and Lucy Conray, who owned him, his brother Wash, his parents Jodora and Victor and somewhere in the neighborhood of twenty other slaves. He had no memory of who might have played it, only that it sat in the house undisturbed for years after the slaves had been freed. When he and his mama finally moved off the land and onto a small strip of their own, it was one of only a handful of things he took with him. The story sounded reasonable except for one minor detail. Art swore that he had been born on the Conray farm in the year 1848. That he had been a young man when the Union army sent four soldiers up from Houston who read aloud from a piece of paper saying all of the slaves were free to go. That he had stood in front of the big house there and watched as J.T. and Lucy tossed a few bags onto a wagon and rode away, leaving the workers there on the land for the next couple of years, until a rainy season dealt the final blow to the cotton and forced everyone to move off in search of better fortunes. This made Art Conray Patton 109 years old.

"I'm an old man," he said. "I've been transfigured."

Even fresh out of the Angelina River, he didn't look half his age.

4: THE DOCHES GAZETTE

Saw mills. Banks and stores and restaurants wouldn't hire a negro in the 1950s, not in Nacogdoches, not in just about all of east Texas, but every community had at least one saw mill and usually more. Some were saw mill towns. Towns that sprung up around the saw mills instead of the other way around. And almost every one of these saw mills, in turn, had a juke joint somewhere in the near vicinity. A place where workers could relax after work and have a few drinks, play cards, trade stories and listen to music. Negro musicians made meager livings by traveling between these saw mills and playing either in the jukes or at parties. It was at a juke joint called The Pepper Pot, close to Kelty's, that I first ran into Art

Patton. It was also where I first laid eyes on that gourd banjo.

"Strum it," Art said, holding it out with the playing side facing me.

I raked my finger across the four strings, which buzzed like the gourd was full of bees.

"See what I tell you?"

I was writing for the Doches Gazette, a small colored newspaper out of Nacogdoches. Once a bi-monthly, it had just been cut back to a monthly edition. It took so little of my time and brought in so little money that I could scarcely call it a job. Most of my writing consisted of letting the community know who was visiting which relative in which town and who had come to town visiting family. I wasn't breaking big stories, but I was hoping to eventually get some kind of fellowship to go to Wisely College or maybe Prairie View, study to be a real newspaper reporter.

I was at the office one afternoon, waiting around to ask for extra assignments, when an albino named Whitey came in. Whitey was a regular. Homeless and usually jobless, he mainly showed up when he was looking for a little money. Not that he would ever accept a handout. He was always ready to do some sweeping or window washing or whatever you had to do but didn't want to do.

"Got you a big story," he said. "Down in the Sawmill Quarter."

Whitey was touched in the head but he didn't talk

nonsense. I liked him all right.

"Ain't nothing much good ever come out of the Sawmill Quarter," I said.

I figured either someone had cut a limb off, which happened on a regular enough basis that it wasn't really that big of a story, or two workers had gotten into it over a woman or something and someone had been knifed.

"You know The Pepper Pot?" he said.
The odds just got worse.

"Whitey," I said, "trouble at The Pepper Pot quit being news a long time ago."

"Ain't nothing happened at The Pepper Pot," he said, "something about to happen."

That was an angle I hadn't thought of. And that was enough to pique my interest.

5: THE PEPPER POT

Artillery Conray Patton.

The name was scribbled across the bottom of a Nehi Root Beer box. I had never known The Pepper Pot to sell anything other than real beer or whiskey. Jay Henry Britt, who ran the place, said even bourbon and scotch was too fancy for his tastes, and so he wouldn't stock it.

I had been in The Pepper Pot a few times, mostly meeting friends and listening to music, so it wasn't that out of the ordinary for me to show up. I ordered a Dixie beer in a cup and grabbed a seat close to the stage, which consisted of a piece of plywood balanced on six plastic buckets. The Pepper Pot was unusual in that it had any stage at all. Most of the joints in the area pushed a table or two out of the way, just enough to make room for the musicians to crowd in with their instruments.

Whitey hadn't told me much about Art. He said he was old. Real old. So when he walked up to the stage and climbed aboard, holding the banjo in one hand and a bottle of whiskey in the other, I mistook him for someone else. He seemed kind of ageless. Maybe forty, maybe sixty, but probably not far outside either of those points. He had a kind smile, even if his eyes seemed to hold too much sadness.

With most of the musicians who came through the area, what you got was second hand blues. If you were lucky, somebody doing his version of Lightnin' Hopkins. Smokey Hogg. Even old stuff like Blind Lemon Jefferson. Not many were playing their own songs. None were doing what Art did.

"My name is Artillery Conray Patton, but you may call me Art," he said. "It's good to be back home."

The next three hours was a ride I'll never forget. At times, I almost forgot I was inside The Pepper Pot. In fact, the place had more in common with the little churches in the area than one might expect. The one room building, painted white inside and out, the rows of chairs, the stage area, the music. At times, it seemed that the Spirit descended on the place, and I don't mean the alcohol variety. I was riveted.

6: BROWN WORLD

"You may call me Art. For a long time, that's all I was. Sum total all. Art. Something to call me so I would come running when I was supposed to come running, cower when I was supposed to cower. You understand. Come running when I was supposed to come running, cower when I was supposed to cower. Something to differentiate me from the others who looked just like me. I know you know what I'm saying. Something to differentiate me. Like a dog. Like you would call a dog. Bonny. Bull. Art.

"Now a dog will look for something good even in the foot that kicks it. That's the way God made a dog. I knew there wasn't much good on that goddamn cotton farm. I didn't have to look far or hard to know that much. Not much good in Patton Landing, back in that time. Sure as hell wasn't no Pepper Pot. And there sure as hell wasn't much good in J.T. Conray. Might have been something there in Lucy Conray or my momma Jodora, or even my friend Jube, if I had been taught to recognize it. If I had been taught to recognize it. I had only been taught to run and to cower. I could see, but I had learned not to think long on anything I saw."

Art seemed content with what he had said and turned his attention to that banjo, which had been thrumming like a piston engine in his hands, just waiting for him to crank it up and take off. Which is pretty much what he did. The banjo didn't sound like any banjo I had ever heard. It was run through a small Valco Supro amplifier and cranked up until it all hummed with electric current. I halfway expected sparks to shoot out of the banjo.

"The whole world seemed brown back then," he said. "The whole world seemed brown.

"Maybe it's the memories that have browned. All of the people around me, the clothes we wore, the dirt beneath our feet, the buildings, the fields we worked, the mules, even the sky appeared a dirty burlap color, the stars poking through where it had been rubbed threadbare."

The banjo notes jabbed and slashed away like they were stabbing holes in the air. It was getting hard to breathe. Suddenly, his right hand flailed against the strings, and, just when you thought the strings were about to snap, the tension did instead. The air seemed to cool.

"Me and Jube were laying on hay bales one early evening, just outside the big barn, and there were already enough stars to work out a couple of patterns."

He wasn't singing, but he wasn't not singing. The words seemed to roll out of something deep inside of him, like water.

"Now Jube's daddy, he drove the mule cart down to the riverboats and back. Did you know riverboats used to come right up this river, right up to Pattonia? Big steamboats come to bring coffee and sugar, salt and flour, tools and cloth. Take away cotton. Bales and bales of it. Three hundred, four hundred bales."

By this time, I had taken the notepad out of my back pocket and was hurriedly taking down notes, most of them in a shorthand only I would be able to decipher.

"Jube's daddy, he had shown us some of the different constellations, and we were eager to try it for ourselves. We were eager to try it out for ourselves. After a full day's work, though, I tell you what. It was hard to keep our minds on it. At least, it was for me. My head was buzzing with the heat of the day or maybe it was cicadas. You still got cicadas around here? Still got them goddamn cicadas. Can't get rid of 'em. Well, my head was buzzing good. Maybe the way some of y'all's is buzzing, I don't know. It was hard to keep from slipping off into sleep, and that's exactly what I did. Exactly what I did. I ain't lying When I woke up, said when I woke up, Jube was gone. He was long gone. And music had already started up just around the back of the quarters."

Well, that was when he slid off into the old slave song "Follow The Drinking Gourd."

The riverbank will make a very good road,
the dead trees show you the way,
Left foot, peg foot, traveling on,
Follow the drinking gourd.
Where the great big river meets the little river,
Follow the drinking gourd,
The old man is awaiting
for to take you to freedom,
If you follow the drinking gourd.

The way he was stomping his foot on the plywood stage, I was afraid it was about to buck up and splinter. Maybe he saw that too, because he brought it all back down.

"Ladies and gentlemen."

That's what he said, even though I don't think there was a lady within half a mile of The Pepper Pot.

"Ladies and gentlemen, I remember I looked up into the sky that night and saw that Big Dipper, its handle pointing the way, sure as the world, toward the evening star. Sure as the world it was. I never will forget. I was about to push myself to my feet, just about to push myself up, when there was suddenly a split in the sky. I'm telling you there was a split in the sky like two parts of a curtain pulling apart. Can't you see? There was a flash of light— quiet, like some kind of heat lightning— and then I seen a man's face."

The music had pulled back to where it was mostly just hum, like an electric wave washing over the room and then ebbing to reveal more words.

"Not the face of a God or angel as I'd seen in Sunday books, but a normal face like that of Mister Conray or Mister Patton, looking down at me."

Wave and ebb.

"The man had a startled, almost angry, expression as if I was gazing on him in the bath or some private endeavor. Then he reached and pulled the curtain around him. He reached and pulled the curtain around him and was gone..."

7: A GLIMPSE OF SOMETHING TRUER

The music gone momentarily, along with the man in the sky, Art Patton sat on the stool and talked to the half dozen of us who had formed a half-circle around him.

"You know, I told this to my mother, Jodora. My mother's name was Jodora. I told it to my friend Jube. I even told Mrs. Lucy. That's Mrs. Lucy Conray, the lady who owned me and my family. Only one who didn't laugh accused me of drinking from one of Mister Conray's moonshine jars. Y'all know about them moonshine jars. Jay Henry probably got one he'll sell you. They all dismissed me, every single one of 'em. But you know what, I don't think I even knew how to tell a lie back then. I don't think I even knew

20

how. I know I never ever forgot what I saw, and that ain't no lie. I continued on, going to the Sunday school, but I would no longer hold any belief in the stories they told us there. I was convinced I had been given a glimpse of something truer."

He looked down and flipped his banjo in his hands, rubbing the gourd with his palm like it would bring him good fortune.

"It put an effect on the whole rest of my days, right up until all those other people were long gone dead and buried. Yes sir, it did. Until all the people around me were gone and buried, and I was the last old man living in Pattonia."

He strummed an open chord.

"But that, as they say, is another story."

8: WHY I DON'T TAKE REQUESTS

"When I was seventy-six years old, a white man named George Delafield—— who lived right here in Pattonia, although there wasn't really any Pattonia left to speak of— died and left almost everything he owned to me. To me. Artillery Conray Patton.

"Now George Delafield and I had spent a good portion of the last fifteen or twenty years playing four card stud and forty-two and swapping the same stories back and forth. Back and forth. Still, it might have made less sense, him bequeathing his entire estate to a colored man four years older than he himself, if there had been anyone else left alive to claim it.

"As it was, there was George and me living in

houses on either end of Pattonia Road, the colored nurse who tended to George and lived with her two kids down on the county highway, and about one hundred and thirty dead souls in the Mount Violet Eastview Cemetery. One hundred and thirty dead souls in Mount Violet Eastview. I expect there's a few more out there nowadays. At that time, I was the only one left. The only one left. I had managed to bore everybody in Pattonia to death.

"Harmon Littlejohn, who lived in Oak Ridge, halfway between Patton Landing and Marion's Ferry, was the only other face I saw on a regular enough basis to know it. Harmon played blues and old-timey music at saw mill and paper mill camps around the area under the name Little John Harmon, because he said people could remember it better. When he was down on his luck, Harmon lived in the old seed store on the main road through Pattonia. The old store has literally gone to seed, but it's still there. Anyway, Harmon lived there in George Delafield's seed store whenever he was down on his luck. I had never seen a man so down on his luck. I mean down.

"Harmon went with me to the funeral home just south of Nacogdoches when George Delafield passed. I went into town as seldom as possible, just about always on Saturdays and sticking close to the Church Street area, what the whites called Nigger Main. Do they still call it Nigger Main? George, he was dead as a wagon tire and wouldn't have known if they had rolled him right through the town square, but I had promised that I would try to see to it he was buried in Mount Violet. What seemed like an easy enough request at the time proved not to be."

Art looked down at my table and saw me scratching into my notepad.

"You taking notes out there, better take this down. What seems like an easy enough request don't always prove to be. That's why I don't take requests."

The whole room seemed to laugh, which made me realize how many of the patrons were listening to every word he said. Art stopped talking and concentrated on the music for a minute, coaxing out sounds I'd never heard from a banjo. I decided it needed another name. This was definitely not banjo music.

"This ain't no nigger funeral home."
He flattened his voice into a hillbilly drawl that made a good portion of us snap our necks around.

"The man high-stepping across the lot toward me and Harmon was in no shape to fight. I can tell you that. Fatter than both of us put together and stuffed into the cleanest white suit you ever saw, he was talking faster than I could keep up with and walking even faster."

Art puffed out his chest and stomped his feet in time, like he was marching off into battle.

"The veins were standing out on his forehead, I tell you what. I wasn't sure if it was due to that tight suit, the physical exertion of coming to meet me and Harmon, or the idea of having two niggers sullying his establishment."

When he said the word nigger, he slashed out at his banjo and made a fierce racket.

"Harmon immediately backed up to our wagon. Yes sir, he backed up and gave my old mule Zeus a nervous slap on the back."

He popped the head of the banjo with the back of his fist.

"The man come within ten feet of me and stopped."

The music came to a standstill. Silence.

"I know you know what come next."

The music strummed back to life.

"You hear me?" he said. "We don't serve you people. You need to go on into town. Go on into town, head out east past the main square. That's where your people do business."

Orton Hill. Orton Hill on East main in Nacogdoches. Where I still did business to that very day. Where all the negro business was done. I almost felt embarrassed. As if I had suddenly become a witness. As if I had become a character in the story. It was something I had no desire for.

"I took off my hat and looked down, careful to avoid the man's eye."

I looked down at my notes and pretended to write.

"I understand you've got my friend George Delafield in there."

Dellafeel, I wrote, with a question mark.

"Man spit a wad of snuff at the ground, right where my gaze had fallen. Said you work for Mister Delafield?"

He stretched the words this way and that, like they were saltwater taffy.

"I shook my head. No sir, he was a friend. I looked up and watched the man scratch his head and wipe his brow. His skin was so red it looked almost purple, specially up against that white suit."

Scattered laughter.

"You boys ain't from around here, are you? I nodded yes. Then I shook my head no. I nodded yes. Then I shook my head.

"We're from Pattonia."

9: WE DON'T EAT NO SEED

"He didn't seem to know where Pattonia was at or have any desire to learn it. Didn't seem to have a clue that it was right down the road a few miles.

"The service is tomorrow morning at ten, he said."

Art lowered himself into a whisper. He was still working that hillbilly voice, but it was now a hillbilly whisper.

"It won't hurt none for you to come in quiet and stand along the back."

A few men standing along the back, where the card tables lined a wall that was covered in beer and cigarette ads, threw out a few catcalls.

"I told him that George and I had said our

proper goodbyes, and I wasn't there to request any such privilege."

He played for several bars, seemingly deep in thought. Or maybe deep into the music. It was hard to tell. When he looked up, he seemed surprised to see us all still listening. He smiled.

"I explained as briefly as I could how the Delafields had run the seed store in Pattonia for over sixty years, and that when there wasn't hardly any Pattonia left. See, everyone in George's family had either died off or moved off. Mostly they had all died. Old George had continued to run that seed store until finally there wasn't anybody but me and young Harmon Littlejohn left.

"Me and Zeus here, we don't eat no seed and neither does my friend Harmon, I said."

The place seemed to shake with laughter. I didn't know how to write what it felt like to be in there at that moment.

"I told that peckerwood that during our final game of forty-two, I had promised George Delafield— that dead white man you got in your building right there— that I would do whatever I could to see that he was properly buried in Mount Violet, where his wife Carrie is buried as well as their young daughter Lovey. Y'all can go out there and see if I'm lying. I wasn't lying to that white man, and I'm not gonna lie to y'all.

"I'm sympathetic to your little story, the white man in the tight white suit said. However, seeing that you're most certainly not family, I'm not free to just hand the body over. What you need to do is get somebody from Mister Delafield's family to make that kind of request."

I laughed to myself. I had never been in that position before, and yet I had. Hadn't we all been.

"I reminded him of the part in the story where there was no family left that wasn't already buried in Pattonia."

Art shook his head in mock disgust.

"If that's true, he said, you'll need to take it up with the local authority."

He leaned into his microphone and worked the last word over really hard, stretching it out.

"The local authority?"

"The local....authority."

The music was working its own magic, repeating itself until it became like the snake eating its own tail. I couldn't tell where one line began and the next ended. If I concentrated on it, I was missing part of the story. If I got up to buy another drink, I was missing part of the story. I couldn't move.

"Just who exactly is the local authority? Harmon said to me.

"By this time, Harmon was sitting on the wagon looking at a copy of Just So Stories that we'd dug up in the back of the seed store. I had convinced Harmon to teach himself to read so he could write down all of the songs he made up. He played long songs. Lots of words. Lots and lots of words. Kind of

29

like this one."

I had never seen a musician have the patrons of The Pepper Pot so completely in the palm of his hand.

"I don't know who the local authority is, I said. I was too afraid to ask."

I saw Jay Henry Britt behind the bar. Even he was laughing.

"I climbed up next to him into that old wagon and grabbed the lines.

"Haw!"

I watched his fingers on the strings. It seemed like he couldn't hit a wrong note if he tried. It was as if his fingers had a mind all their own.

"I drove old Zeus out of the lot, tipping my hat to a passing group of young children.

"I'll be surprised if there's three people at that funeral tomorrow, Harmon said.

I said...and that's counting George."

10: NOTHING TO COMPLAIN ABOUT

"There was no way I was going to tangle with any Nacogdoches law. Everybody knew the story of them hanging a colored man there in the town square. They'd given him a trial too, they said, so the hanged man had nothing to complain about."

How long ago was he talking about? I couldn't be sure. I wondered how long Chief of Police C.E. Battle had been in power, imposing his curfew on the colored population, patrolling our neighborhoods and shaking down anyone he happened to come across that didn't look just right.

"Hanged man didn't have nothing to complain about."

I was laughing, but I couldn't say why.

"At best, they might throw you in the back of the jail and forget you were there until someone come along and reminded 'em."

He stopped talking and played, the thumb on his fretting hand wrapping over the top of the banjo neck to grab the bass notes. I wondered how long he'd been playing. And why he had chosen a banjo instead of a guitar.

"No, there was enough trouble in the world. No need in Art Patton asking for extra. Me and Harmon went back home with the sun falling into the trees to the right. As the moon came up on the left, I wondered if there were people up there."

There were only two windows in The Pepper Pot. I looked out, almost expecting to see the moon right there. All I could see were pine trees, but there was a hint of green to them, which let me know there was a moon spilling down on them from somewhere.

"As the moon came up, I wondered if there were people up there on it looking back at us, or if the people up there could even make out enough to know we were down here."

11: MOMMA SAID IT WAS WISE

I wanted to thank Whitey. Not because I could see any big story in Art Patton, but because I had never heard music like that. It wasn't the blues. At least, it wasn't any kind of blues that I could pin down. It didn't have the twelve-bar form. The repetition had no set formula at all. There was no rhyme or reason to any of it, and yet it mesmerized in the same way that Lightnin' Hopkins' best stuff did. Or like good gospel music. It seemed to bring the dark and the light together in a way that made a complete picture. I wanted to see more.

Sitting where I was, it was hard to see the room filling up behind me, until people started moving to the other two tables near the stage. It wasn't unusual that the crowd would get bigger as the night went on, but usually the stage tables would slowly make their ways back to the side, away from the music, to where people could sit and talk and hear themselves curse as they lost their week's pay. So tonight was a little different.

"Who the fuck are you?"

Sam Bolden had arrived and taken a table directly across from me. From the looks of things, he was already liquored up when he walked through the door. He was loud and boisterous from having to shout over the saw at Spurlin Tie and Timber, where he was a foreman. People pointed to him as one of the most successful colored men in the Nacogdoches area. They also pointed to him for less savory reasons.

"My name is Art. For a long time, that's all it was. We're talking about a long time ago. Even before you was born. Even before the war. We never knew anything about the war until it was already halfway over. We never knew what the fighting was for until the Union army sent four soldiers up from Houston who read aloud from a piece of paper saying all of the slaves were free to go. I didn't know what a slave was. I had never heard the word. I didn't know what they meant when they said I was free. It was like telling Bonny the hound dog she now was free to speak her mind."

He wasn't talking about World War II. He wasn't even talking about the Spanish-American War. He was talking about the Civil War.

"Funny enough, it was J.T. and Lucy Conray who packed up their suitcases and left Pattonia. A good portion of the workers had nowhere to go and didn't know how to get there if they did. Me and my family stayed there on the farm for another year or more, until finally a hard rain season came and the cotton played out. Then we moved a few miles closer to Lufkin."

There were more catcalls, Lufkin being an arch enemy in football in both the colored and the white schools.

"You gotta understand. By that time, we all knew that Nacogdoches was chock full of Confederates. Angry sons of bitches who would be reminded why they were angry every time they laid eyes on my black skin. Lufkin, it was said, was full of Yankee sympathizers. We believed it too, because we had seen more than one white farmer from Nacogdoches literally spit the words from his mouth and wipe them on his shirt sleeve. You know how white people in Nacogdoches hate the people in Lufkin? Now you know why. Now you what it all goes back to. I wouldn't lie to you. Why would I lie?"

People were talking, but no one brought forth an answer. Everyone was really starting to wonder where this guy had come from. And what his purpose was. It seemed like he had a good bit more on his mind than music.

"It was about the time we moved off the farm that I took the name Art Conray. Named myself after the people who had once owned me. That's what lots of us did. Named ourselves after the people who had owned us and worked us and all-too-often beat us within an inch of our lives. Momma said it was wise. Momma said it was wise because I had an older brother and cousins who had been sold to plantation owners somewhere off in Louisiana, and the Conray name would make it easier for them to find us. If they even cared to find us. If they were even still alive."

"There are still Conrays around here," a man sitting with Sam Bolden said. "You connected to any of them?"

"I'm bound to be. Bound to be."

"The colored Conrays or the white Conrays?"

"Take your pick, sir. Take your pick. After a while, I decided my brother Wash wasn't coming back. I didn't want to be known by that name. The name of Conray. I amended my name with the place that I called home just in time for the 1870 census. That was the first time the government man come around wanting to know who we were and where we were from. I told that man I was Art Patton. He said, did I have a middle name. I told him my name was Art Conray Patton. That's what he wrote down. That's the way I finally became the man I was to be. Art Conray Patton. Born at the age, I think I was twenty-one years old. As Chaucer says, better late than never."

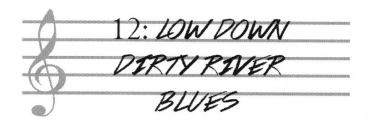

12: LOW DOWN DIRTY RIVER BLUES

"The seed store seemed to miss George Delafield as much as we did. George hadn't been there in months, ever since he'd been bitten by the hookworm. Yes sir, he was bitten by the hookworm, and then that fever had set in. Once that fever set in, we never saw him 'round the seed store anymore.

"When George gets back, we would say, knowing that he wasn't coming back but still thinking that he could. Knowing that he wasn't but thinking that he could."

Art seemed to like something in the sound of that and sang it a few times, a different way every time, as if he was looking at it from different angles.

"It was enough to keep the store front swept

clean and a stack of wood propped next to the stove, even when winter turned to spring and the weather warmed up again. You know what I mean? When George gets back, we best have this place swept up and looking good.

"I taught Harmon to play forty-two, but he never did get the hang of gin rummy or poker. He were to come in here, some of you motherpluggers would take him to the cleaners I'm saying he would have a long night. All the same, he graduated from those Just So Stories to Treasure Island which he didn't care for and quickly traded for Huckleberry Finn.

"This book talks the way I do, he said.

"All right, all right, I said. Play me some of them low down dirty river blues, Nigger Jim."

And off Art went into some real gut bucket blues. The kind you didn't hear much anymore. And he was making that banjo bend and moan like a guitar. I had to look again to make sure he hadn't switched it out.

"Harmon had moved up into the store for good, it seemed, only going home to wash up and pack for a trip up to Marshall or Malakoff to play at a dance or something. They still have dances up in Malakoff? They used to know how to throw a party up that way."

He played a few measures and thought.

"Harmon Littlejohn— otherwise known as Little John Harmon— had taken off on just such a trip, and I was sitting in the kitchen of my house, like the last bullet in the gun, when I heard this sputter and rumble approaching."

He almost sounded like a preacher if you didn't take notice of the bad words.

"I knew what it was. Yes sir, I knew. Even if I had never seen an automobile on Pattonia Road, I'd seen them in town. I was at the screen door just in time to see it pull into the yard and sputter to a stop."

The music fell silent.

"Artillery Patton? You in there?

"I looked over at the hunting rifle propped against the wall.

"Yes sir."

Cue the music.

"That man jumped out his car like he thought it might explode any moment and made a beeline for my porch, stopping suddenly when he reached the first step. He was a white man with a red tint to his hair and a mustache the fell down his chin on each side. He wore a suit but it looked like a suit that might come out of the back of my closet."

Art laughed loud and shook his head, shaking the banjo again while he was at it.

"You are Artillery Conway Patton?

"Conray, I said, but, yes sir, that'll do."

That white man looked down at a roll of papers in his hand and nodded to himself.

"What you want with me? I said.

"I wanted to know what caused him to come all the way out here in his little motor car. What made him run at my porch like he thought the damn thing was about to blow sky high. He braced his foot against the first porch step, and this is what he said..."

Art leaned over into his mic again and paused just long enough for most of the people in front of the stage to lean in toward him.

"I'm part of a law firm in Nacogdoches, and we need you to come into town."

The crowd inside The Pepper Pot groaned.

"Yes, we need you to come into town and talk to us. Sign some papers.

"Oh lord, what had I done. What on God's green earth had I gone and done now.

"I can talk just fine right here, I said."

The crowd hooted and clapped their hands.

"Man handed me a piece of paper. I turned it over in my hands and looked at it real close. Law Office Of Lester Massey. It said, Law Office of Mister Lester Massey. His name was big and fancy looking. Not like him at all. he wasn't too big, and he sure wasn't fancy. I looked down at the bottom of the card. Pilar Street, Nacogdoches.

"Uh oh, I said. What on God's green earth did I do?

"That peckerwood laughed at me.

"Mister Patton, you've done nothing, he said. Absolutely nothing.

"I was thinking, well then, what did I not do that I was supposed to do?"

Howls of laughter from everyone, it seemed.

Myself included.

"Mister Patton, this is about settling up the matter of a George Demetrius Delafield."

Art seemed to let out a big sigh, and the music did the same.

"It was the first time a white man had ever called me Mister in my life."

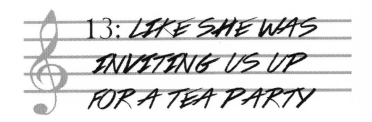

13: LIKE SHE WAS INVITING US UP FOR A TEA PARTY

"I was regretting any promises I had made to poor old George. When I died, I decided, they could lock the doors and shut the windows and let my house be my grave. A humorous thought until I realized how likely it was to happen. It might be another hundred years before anyone came back down the road to find me. Except for Harmon. Harmon showed up two days later.

Malakoff sent him back with a small roll of bills and half a jug of corn liquor.

"Half a jug? I said.

"Some of it sloshed out on the way home, he said.

"Maybe some of y'all know what that's all about."

My cup had sloshed itself empty, and I was ready for a refill. I could see a little wiggle room at the end of the bar and decided to make my move. Walking away from the music, I was surprised to find business as usual at both the card tables and the bar. The music nothing more than background noise. Art's voice hanging just above it like cigarette smoke.

Jay Henry saw me and sent a young man over to help me. I ordered up another Dixie and mentioned that the musician was good tonight. I mean, really good.

"That right?" the guy said. "I can't even tell if he's talking in English."

He poured more beer into the same cup and took my money.

"So Harmon finally talked me into going into town the next morning. He figured somebody wanted some money to cover burial costs. Hell, we didn't even know where George was. What they'd done with him. Maybe they were waiting for me to come pick him up. I didn't know.

"We may as well find out where they put him, Harmon said, so we'll know where to pay our respects.

"Now, paying respects was one thing. Paying for the funeral or burial was a whole other matter. Still, Harmon grabbed up his roll of money, and I got the card the lawyer left with me, and off we went."

He ventured off into some blues refrain about going to town. Seemed like a T-Bone Walker song.

Something I had heard before. The banjo strings squealed under his fingers, throwing out harmonics that sounded like some ghostly harmonica blowing along.

"I knew where Pilar Street was, so I took a different route into town than usual, coming in directly from the south.

"You sure we should be coming along this way? Harmon said.

"Harmon didn't know the neighborhood, but he knew it was white. Of course, it being white and all, that was exactly why he didn't know it.

"Watch this, I said."

He choked the music down into a half-time stomp.

"I slowed old Zeus down and pulled to the side of the road just as we approached a great big two-story farmhouse surrounded by a pretty little white fence and the brightest green lawn you ever saw. I went to pointing on up at the house. I almost had to make Harmon look.

"I said, looky yonder, Harmon.

"Way up on the big wrap-around porch, up on top of that hill with its green grass, sitting pretty behind that little picket fence was an equally pretty white lady. She was an old lady, but she was sure enough pretty. And just as white as that picket fence that kept me away from her."

Sam Bolden looked at me and shook his head.

"Well, that old white lady stood up and started

waving like she was inviting us up for a tea party. Why would I lie to you about a thing like that? That's exactly what she did. Harmon, poor Harmon hid his face in his hat."

"That'll still get you killed nine times out of ten," Sam Bolden said.

"Harmon said, What in the hell are you doing, Art?

"Zeus kept his eyes on the road, and Harmon tried his best to do the same.

"Just smile and wave, I said. Just smile and wave."

14: THAT DOOR AINT GONNA OPEN ITSELF

"The showy writing on Lester Massey's card didn't match up with his office, a small clapboard building two blocks off the main square in town. We passed it by twice, looking for some clue that we were at the right place. Finally, Harmon spied a small sign on the door with Massey's name across it, in a poor attempt to copy the penmanship on the piece of paper in my hand. We tied Zeus to a post and approached the door.

"Should we rap on it or call out his name? I said.

"Harmon said, I'm doing neither.

"I stood there and sized up my options. More like I was trying to summon up my courage. I finally decided I could call out his name one time, and if he chose not to answer, we could unhitch Zeus and maybe head down to Nigger Main for a shave and a haircut. Maybe a matinee movie.

"Mister Massey, sir, I called out."

It was a quiet kind of call, if his telling of it was accurate. You could hear it, but only if you were cupping your ear and concentrating.

"Just about like that. Mister Massey, sir.

"You can stand there all day. That door ain't gonna open itself. I jumped and turned around, and there stood Mister Massey right behind us, no further than you are to me."

Art nodded his head in my direction. I nodded politely back.

"This is a place of public business, he said. Just open the door and step inside.

"I did as he suggested. The office was one room. Didn't even have a closet to hang a jacket in. There were four windows, one on each wall. Two of them had been propped open to create a blow through. A desk with one busted up chair behind it and another in front that was in even worse shape.

"Take a seat, Mister Patton.

"I elbowed Harmon and mouthed it. Mister Patton.

"There some kind of trouble? Harmon said.

"He seemed happy to be standing, a position which put him closer to the door, closer to getting out in the event that things turned bad. I was close enough to an open window

47

"Massey fell into his chair, which somehow survived the invasion. He shifted around in it and pulled a cabinet full of papers right out into his lap, licking his thumb and fingering through them from back to front and then back again."

All this time, Art was playing up and down the strings of his banjo, the rhythm of his hands matching the words.

"Back to front and then back again.

"My lands, he said. I was looking up Patton. He said, it's Delafield that I'm trying to find here.

"I cleared my throat.

"Uhmm, I had asked if Mister Delafield might be buried in Mount Violet in Patton Landing, I said. That's where all his people are at.

"Massey looked up at Harmon and then at me.

"George Delafield has already been buried here in the city.

"That's when Harmon reached into his pocket. Yes sir, he reached down into his pocket and pulled out that roll of money.

"How much would it cost to have his body moved? Harmon said. I have seven dollars to put down on it.

"Massey stood half way up, laughed, lost his balance and fell back into place. The chair was obviously stronger than it appeared.

"Boy, I'm sure it would cost a bit more than that. However, if you're that concerned about it, I just might be in a position to help you."

Art seemed like he had gone back in time. I could almost see him in the little office. I wondered if we could open up the windows in The Pepper Pot. See what kind of blow through we could get going. Things were beginning to heat up.

"I stood up, no longer feeling comfortable in the chair with Harmon standing at my side and Massey going up and down like he was.

"I'm not sure that's something we can think about right now, I said.

"I didn't figure George would like the thought of Harmon's Malakoff money buying his eternal home any more than I did. I was just about ready to excuse myself from the proceedings.

"I have George Delafield's last will and testament right here, Mister Patton. I think you might be interested in having a look see."

"Goddamn right," said the man sitting next to Sam Bolden. "Let's have a look."

He slammed his fist down on the table, their drinks jumping in response.

"He fanned the pages across his desk like a hand of playing cards. He must have seen the resemblance too.

"Massey looked across the table at me and said, You've got yourself a winning hand right here. Yes indeed, boy. a winning hand.

"I sat back down and picked up the first card in the stack."

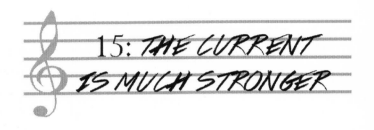

15: THE CURRENT IS MUCH STRONGER

"How fucking old are you?"

Sam Bolden had had enough of Art Patton's stories, and he'd had enough whiskey to say so.

"Well, how old are you, sir?" said Art. He either didn't recognize the edge in Bolden's voice or just decided to pay it no mind.

Bolden was standing up, not twelve feet away from the stage. He was probably unsteady enough that I could have tipped him over, but the last thing we needed was for a fight to break out.

"I was born in 1848, sir," Art said. "I don't rightly know the month of it."

Those must have seemed like fighting words to Sam.

"So you're telling us you're one hundred and fifty years old."

I'm not sure Sam's math skills would have been much better had he been sober. But the drink wasn't helping much.

"Why would I tell you a story if I didn't want you to believe it?" Art said.

Noah McDaniel, who worked for Sam at Spurlin and was undoubtedly trying to score points with his boss, approached the stage from the bar area.

"Do you actually know any real songs?"

Now, the reason Jay Henry Britt served beer in Styrofoam cups was to keep people from using bottles as weapons, but the whiskey came in a glass bottle, and sometimes Jay Henry would even supply shot glasses, if the bottle was being passed around. So when Art laid his banjo to the side and stood up with his whiskey bottle in his right fist, everybody in the joint tensed up. Art took a swig instead of a swing.

"I'm not asking anybody to believe in a half told story," he said. "But yes sir, I know some songs. I know a whole bunch of songs."

He sat back down and picked up the banjo.

"What time is it?" he said. "Is it one o'clock yet?"

It was just after midnight, not yet one. The moon had moved on, leaving the pine trees to their darkness. The Pepper Pot was a beating heart inside of a dead body.

Art played through the first two lines before I recognized what he was playing. Blind Lemon

51

Jefferson's "Electric Chair Blues." It was a song I had known for several years, but, up close and personal, its ferocious undercurrent was frightening. Art sang it slow and down low, like he knew someone was going to flip the switch as soon as it ended. He repeated phrases, entire verses, until they became a prayer for deliverance.

I wonder why they electrocute a man
at the one o'clock hour of night
   Said I wonder why they electrocute a man
at the one o'clock hour of night
Because the current is much stronger
when folks has turned out all the lights

All too soon, the night came to an end, Jay Henry turned out the lights, and everyone was left to make their way back home, leaving Patton's Landing Road empty and going nowhere. I tried to find Art Patton. I wanted to thank him. I wanted to ask for a little more time. Somehow, he slipped off through the back door and into the night. Was there a waiting car? An accomplice somewhere on the grounds? I never found out.

I returned to the Gazette and went back to work writing about families moving this way and that, coming into the community and then leaving it. All the time, the notebook sat on my desk, turned to another page. I asked around, and no one seemed to know anything about Art Patton. I drove out to see Jay Henry, and he had little information.

"He said he was one of the Pattons that use to

live out here," Jay Henry said. "You might try to look them up."

I tried to find Whitey, but he had gone missing. Not unusual there.

As the days went by, my hunger to find out more only grew. I decided to use a few connections and see what I could turn up. Maybe this was all just a part of the story.

16: SORRY FOR WHAT?

It took a week but I was able to find a copy of the 1870 census in the courthouse. It covered all of Nacogdoches County, but I found Pattonia at the bottom of the last page, above only Saints Rest. I was surprised by how many people lived in Pattonia. Four or five hundred people in an area where only one or two families now lived.

The lady behind the counter didn't want to give me access to any records. At first, she didn't even want me in the building. I had to use a side door. I had to stand at the back. I had to wait until all of the white customers had been dealt with. If she thought I would give up and leave, she was mistaken. At last, she allowed me to look through their books, but only after I made her think I was trying to trace family.

"The name?" she said.

"Conray."

She stopped flipping through the book.

"Most of the Conrays around here are white."

I nodded. I would say she eyed me with suspicion, but she had already been doing that. Now it became a glare.

"I thought you were looking for family."

She was speaking loud enough that another lady who was typing away on a typewriter stopped to listen in. It made me self-conscious. I lowered my voice, hoping she would get the hint.

"Yes."

"Your own family?" she said. Louder.

I glanced at the lady with the typewriter who quickly resumed her tapping.

"They used to own my family, ma'am," I said.

It was a lie, but a calculated one. A lie brought about by this lady's stubbornness. The suspicion slid from her face as she grasped for something suitable to replace it. She came up with the usual.

"Oh, you poor thing," she said. "I'm sorry."

Sorry for what, I wanted to say. Was she apologizing for her attitude when I walked in? For questioning what valid reason a colored boy might have for walking into her place of business? For making me stand at the back door. Drink water from a separate fountain. Or was she apologizing for hundreds of years of enslaving my people?

I thought about Art's comment. How the Conray family had named him just as they had named their dogs. What were the dog's names? I couldn't remember. But why had the Conrays not let Art's mother name him? What about his father? And would they even be on the census?

She handed me a book, a large black book. One of many on the shelves behind her.

"This is very old, so be extremely careful with it."

She stepped to the side, propped against a wall and waited. Close enough to make sure I did exactly as told. I flipped to the back of the book and started at the end.

17: THE CONRAYS

The Conrays were long gone from Pattonia by 1870, but John Thomas Conray was still listed in land records as owning sixty acres on the southwest end of Patton Landing Road. Seeing his name written into the ledger made Art's stories feel even more alive. Just this one piece of information was enough to drive me further, deeper into the past.

I found out that most of the land where the Conray farm had been located was now owned by Temple Industries, an oil and gas company. There didn't seem to be a way back to the family. I decided to take a drive back out to the area, just to nose around. I didn't tell anybody but my brother Paul where I was going. I knew my parents wouldn't like the idea of me going off toward Woden in the family car, a Dodge '53 Coronet. I tried to get Paul to come along, but he had other plans.

I knew the Patton Landing Road well enough, even if I was more familiar with the east end. The Pepper Pot end. I took off with a few notes, landmarks to look for that might lead me to something identifiable. I figured if I came up totally empty, I could always head for the juke joint and have a beer or two. Maybe ask around if anyone had heard from Art Patton.

Patton Landing Road is almost completely under tree cover. The trees from each side of the road grow over and meet in the middle, making for a green canopy. As a result, the area is always in shade, and, with the river nearby, it's usually a good bit cooler than summer in town.

I parked less than a mile down the road, off the road to Woden, and got out of the car. There was a small tin sign tacked to a fence post announcing that I was stepping onto Temple land. I knew the river snaked just north of the trees and that if I walked back toward the big road, I should be walking right across the old Conray property.

The undergrowth was thick once you got into the trees. It was obvious Temple was doing nothing with their acquisition. At times, it was hard to make progress, and I had to alter my route. As a result, I got more and more off course, and by the time I reached the river, I knew I had backtracked too far.

I had seen an old house back along a fence line, but I knew it wasn't anything from the Conrays. There was a truck parked in front of it and a couple of dogs rustling around. I turned right and headed deeper into the woods, but back in the direction of Patton Landing Road. That's when I stumbled upon the remains of a couple of old cabins. I say remains. One of them had fallen in, but the other was in unusually decent shape. It didn't have a floor, but I knew it probably never did have one. There were no panes in the windows. Again, it's likely there never had been. I was pretty sure I was looking at slave cabins. What Art Patton had called the Quarters.

I pulled the Kodak Brownie from my pocket, a new purchase at the Gazette that I hadn't exactly gotten clearance to take. I snapped a handful of shots, some inside and some out. Vegetation had taken over much of the walls, trying to hide the past from the present day ghosts still inhabiting the area, but all but one of the walls were still standing. The better of the two looked about as inhabitable as the house with the truck and the dogs.

I was pretty sure that, having found a remnant of the slave quarters, I would be able to find something of the main house not too far away. I started off in the direction where I suspected it would be, with the intention of making a circle around the area until I walked up on something else. I quickly discovered an old well and peered down into a blackness that I couldn't see the end of. I remembered Paul telling me how most old wells in the area had skeletal remains at the bottom of them. It gave me a creepy feeling.

Stepping back from the hole, I heard movements coming from the direction of the road. If I had been closer to the old slave houses, I might have either ducked into or behind one, but there was really nowhere to go. I hoped it was a deer. Maybe one of the hunting dogs. Anything but a wild boar or even a bear.

"Oh my God," I heard someone say, "it's a nigger."

I had nothing to shoot anybody with except for a camera.

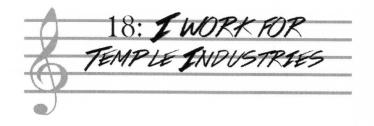

18: I WORK FOR TEMPLE INDUSTRIES

There was only one man, and I knew he had come from the little house I had passed, because he was talking to the two dogs, which were circling around him in opposite directions. He was carrying a rifle, and he was looking right at me. I decided to play friendly.

"How are you doing, sir?"

Ignoring the question, he pointed the rifle back at the two old buildings.

"What you doing, messing around out here, boy?"

The thought flitted through my mind that, if I could make him think I was the ghost of some long dead slave, I might scare the shit out of him and make my way to safety. I also knew it was a good bet he had no idea he was trampling across an old slave plantation. Somehow, the desperation of the moment cleared my mind quickly enough that I even surprised myself.

"I work for Temple Industries," I said. "Temple owns this land, and we're just looking it over."

I hoped he would think I had a partner out there with me. It was all I had to go on. It wasn't the worst thing in the world.

"Temple hiring on niggers now?" he said. "Ain't that a goddamn thing."

I pulled out my camera and showed him.

"Mister Temple sent several of us out to take pictures."

I wasn't sure there even was a Mister Temple. I was hoping the stranger knew as little as I did. What I was really hoping was the stranger was smart enough to know he didn't want Temple Industries discovering one of its employees laying dead less than a quarter mile from his house.

He held the rifle out for me to see, in exchange for my showing him the Brownie.

"I heard some kind of commotion," he said. "I figured I might have me a hog for supper tomorrow night."

I nodded like it never occurred to me he might be looking to kill me.

"I could shoot and dress you," he said. "I don't reckon you'd taste too good."

He thought it was a fine joke. I wasn't convinced.

"My boss might hear the gunshot and come running," I said. "I wouldn't want either one of us getting on his bad side."

That almost seemed to win him over.

"Look, I ain't got nothing against your kind," he said. "Most of 'em come up this way, they've heard those old baby in the well stories. Come nosing around looking for a scare. Well, I can give 'em all of that they want."

I hadn't heard any baby in the well stories. I was as scared as I wanted to be already.

"I expect I got as much in common with you as that big boss man of yours. But if either one of you come around again, trying to buy my little piece of land, I'm liable to grab this here rifle and let it do the talking."

I nodded like I understood more than I did.

"They try to buy your land too?"

He spit on the ground and kicked at it.

"Four times. Each time, he offered me more than the last. But you know what? Sometimes, it ain't about the goddamn money."

I agreed. I honestly agreed with the man.

"This land been in my family going back almost two hundred years," he said.

I wanted to take his picture. There was no way I was ever going to ask him for that.

"You one of the Conrays?" I said.

He cocked his head in a way that made him look

like one of his dogs.

"Bobby Conray the third," he said. "Third and the last."

19: VACATIONING DOWN IN HUNTSVILLE

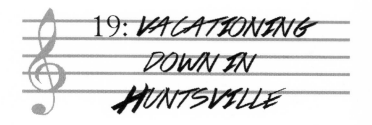

After my encounter with Bobby Conray, I didn't stick around to look for J.T. and Lucy's house. I hightailed it back to the car and drove on down to The Pepper Pot. I was genuinely interested to find out if anyone there had heard from Art Patton, and I was genuinely in need of a beer to steady my nerves.

There was nobody playing that night, but someone had dropped a few nickels in the jukebox, so a Rattlesnake Cooper song was on. Jay Henry got his jukebox serviced from a guy out of Houston, so it was stocked exclusively with artists working on labels down there. That suited me fine. I wasn't a big fan of Memphis and Chicago blues. I stopped by the machine and punched up "Hello Central" by Lightnin'

Hopkins and "Hound Dog" by Big Mama Thornton, one of my new favorites. I ordered a Dixie from Jay Henry and sat at the bar, which I had never done before.

"I've seen you around," he said.

I introduced myself and said I usually turned up for live music but I was in the area.

"Business at Kelty's?"

I guess almost all of their business came from Kelty's, a big lumber yard headed toward Lufkin. Lately, a few houses had spring up in the area, and folks had taken to calling the whole area, although it really wasn't much more than a wide spot in the road, Kelty's. Best I could tell, it was a little bit how Pattonia had once been.

"I was looking for information on the Conray and Delafield families who used to live out here."

Jay Henry nodded and said, "You ought to talk to Hollis Lampkin. His people go way back here."

A man down at the other end of the bar had been pretending not to eavesdrop up until that moment.

"My mother's side of the family knew the Conrays. Most of them have died or moved off long ago."

I had seen the man before. In fact, I was fairly sure he had been there the night Art Patton played. He was dressed in work clothes that looked like they'd never seen soap. Probably stopped off on his way home from Kelty's.

"You heard of a guy named Bobby Conray?"

Jay Henry laughed.

"Bobby Lee. Is he back?'

I decided to hold my cards close to my chest.

"So I heard."

Jay Henry poured himself a drink.

"Bobby Lee's spent the last few years vacationing down in Huntsville."

No more needed to be said. Huntsville was only known for one thing, and that was the state prison that sat right in the middle of it.

"What was he down there for?" I said. Which meant, what was he doing time for.

The man at the end of the bar moved two stools closer and signaled for another cup.

"He's the one that shot those boys in Nacalina several years ago. Never would have gone to the pen if he hadn't bragged to everyone between there and Nacogdoches about it. Some fancy pants D.A. in town decided he would make a name for himself and brought him in for trial."

Jay Henry started to pour a bottle of Pearl into the man's cup, then thought better of it and handed him the bottle. There were only a couple of other people in the place, and nothing seemed to be getting out of hand.

"They sent him down to Huntsville for ten years," Jay Henry said, "and he comes back in three. That comes out to one year per murder."

We all shook our heads and drank our beer, and I

wondered if the boys had been colored boys, but I knew they had been. The premium on white skin would never be so cheap. Before I left, I asked Jay Henry if Art Patton might be playing again sometime, and Jay Henry just said "who?" so I left it at that.

On the way out of the building, a young guy came after me.

"Hey, mister."

He didn't look old enough to be hanging out in a joint like The Pepper Pot, but who was I to judge.

"I hear you say Art Patton?"

I said that he probably did.

"He's playing next Saturday night at the fish fry at the Church of God in Persimmon Grove."

My heart jumped nearly as much as it had when Bobby Conray the Third had come strolling into my view. Bobby Lee.

"Next Saturday night."

"That's right."

"He's singing at a church?" I said.

The boy took a slug from a bottle of Texas Tornado.

"Well, not in the church," he said. "The fish fry is on the outside."

I took out my notebook and jotted the information down. It was getting dark, so I had to write mostly by feel, but it had been a good day. A productive day. I had escaped being murdered by a descendant of the J.T. Conray family.

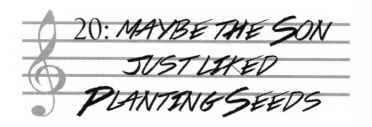

20: MAYBE THE SON JUST LIKED PLANTING SEEDS

Hollis Lampkin lived in Marion's Ferry with his granddaughter and her family. He was eighty-four years old, and, as fortyish year old Hilda said, "he can remember what he ate for breakfast on Christmas morning of 1890. Just don't ask him what he ate for supper last night."

He was bed-ridden and not in good health, but he loved visitors, even if he didn't know them.

Hilda and her son Ted introduced me to him and left us to talk, once it was understood what I had come for.

"So you write for the newspaper," Hollis said. "They hire on colored people now?"

I told him that I wrote for the Doches Gazette, a

small monthly paper for the colored community. I was hoping to write an article having to do with the Patton's Landing area, and had been told that he might remember a few of the families who once lived there.

"I remember just about all of them, I expect," he said. "At least the ones that were there when I was there. And I remember my mother talking about a lot of other ones."

I retrieved my notebook, stretched my fingers and prepared to take notes.

"What did your parents do?"

He thought for a long time, and I wondered if he had heard me, but I think he was preparing his answer before he spoke it.

"My father died when I was very young. He was a slave on the big cotton plantation here, back when all the steamboats were coming up and down the river. They set him free after the war, but he never left Pattonia. I hear 'em call it Patton's Landing nowadays, but back then, it was almost always called Pattonia. I even remember momma talking about the Patton family."

I was writing as quickly as I could, quickly moving to a shorthand that I hoped I would remember later.

"This was the family that the town was named for?"

Hollis nodded.

"It was a town, once upon a time. We had all

kinds of people living here. Stores and even an eating place for a while."

"You remember the seed store that George Delafield used to own?"

He kicked at the sheets on his bed, and I thought that he was going to get up. Hilda scurried in and adjusted things so that his feet were out from under the sheets— "he hates for his feet to get hot," she said— and then disappeared into the other end of the house.

I was about to repeat my question.

"Is the seed store not there anymore?" he said.

I told him that the building was still there, but it had been closed for more than twenty years and had fallen into disrepair.

"Now that building originally belonged to George Delafield's granddaddy," he said. "Was the undertaker place for a long time. There've been more dead bodies in that place than there are in Mount Violet."

"So George took it over after his father retired?"

Hollis deliberated.

"There was a long spell when it was the undertaker and a seed store. I guess either wouldn't enough people die to stay in business, or maybe the son just liked planting seeds more than he liked planting them dead people."

I liked the way Hollis Lampkin talked. I hoped I could get some of his spark into my writing.

"So you would say you know the Delafields

better than you know the Conray family then?" I said.

"I know the Conrays more from hearing my momma talk about them," he said. "They was mostly moved on by the time I was around. Moved down to Beaumont or somewhere I think. She said they got into boating and such. I don't rightly know what they did once they left Pattonia."

I was fascinated. I felt like I was reading a really good book, and I couldn't wait to flip the page and see what happened next.

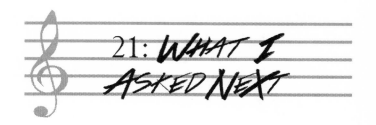

21: WHAT I ASKED NEXT

More to the point, I knew that the book was largely in my hands. What I asked next made all the difference.

"What do you remember your mother saying about the Conrays?"

Again, he waited a long time before speaking.

"Here's what I can recollect. The old man's name was John, but they called him J.T. I even remember why. He had been called John or Big John, and then his wife— whose name, I think, was Lucy or Lucille— had a little boy. I believe they had two boys, but anyhow, this first boy they named Little John. John Junior. What have you. They used to do that a lot.

Everybody in Pattonia knew Little John. The son of the big man. Then, when the little guy was just about schooling age, a terrible sickness came through. Took a handful of people here, a handful there. Some just kids, some fully grown. And that little boy was one of the first to go. They buried him up at Mount Violet. One of the very first headstones put up.

So after that, John didn't want to be called John no more, on account of it reminding him of that little boy. And that's how he came to be J.T."

I took my time, writing it all down, making sure to get it all right. I figured I was giving Hollis more time to think, and that didn't seem to be a bad thing at all.

"What about the slaves?" I said. "Do you remember your mother saying much about all that?"

"That my daddy, who was named Hooker Bill, was a slave there. I think they had a sloosh of them. Well, I say that. They had twelve, maybe fifteen, which was a whole bunch for around here. Of course, that includes little kids too, and them little kids weren't always as productive as they might want them to be."

I decided to cut to the chase.

"Did you ever hear of a slave there named Art? Later, he used the name Art Conray, and then later Art Patton."

Hollis pushed himself up in the bed.

"I knew of an Art Conray, yes sir. If he's the one I'm thinking about, I don't know about him being no slave. He worked construction. I think he worked for somebody over close to Lufkin for a while."

Independent confirmation of Art Conray in the Pattonia area.

"Ain't he the one that killed that little baby?"

That startled me.

"Oh no, I don't think so."

"I guess not," he said.

I almost lost my train of thought.

"Around what time would this have been? The time when you knew the construction worker."

It looked like he was counting to himself.

"I would have to say sometime around 1900, best I can come up with."

"And how old would he have been at that time?"

He didn't hesitate.

"Oh, he was an older man by then. I don't think he was doing much work at that point. Now that I think about it, he for sure was old enough to have been on the Conray farm."

He paused.

"He wasn't old as I am now, I'm telling you. But he was maybe close to sixty."

That seemed to me to be pretty close to the age of the Art Conray I had met. I was seriously beginning to wonder if I had met a ghost. I tried to collect my thoughts and find a way to go forward from there.

"Do you remember if Art Conray played a musical instruments? Was he a musician?"

He kicked his right foot like he was trying to stir up some kind of thought on the subject. Then nothing.

"I have no knowledge of that," he said. "Seems like he might have been the one who lived on that boat. Is he the name of the fellow who lived on that riverboat?"

"I'm not sure," I said.

"If he did, I'm pretty sure he's the one who killed that little baby."

22: GARDNER

On the way out of the house, I asked Hilda if she knew anything about a man killing a baby in Patton's Landing. She said it sounded familiar, but she wasn't sure. Maybe she was thinking about something that had taken place somewhere else.

Any chance she knew how her great-grandfather— Hollis' father— had died? She and Ted were walking me out to my car, and I knew they had other things that needed doing, but I asked anyway.

"He was killed in Nacogdoches," she said.

"The word would be lynched," the boy said.

"Lynched," she said.

Hollis' dad had been working for a fairly well-to-do family in town, and one morning, the mother and a daughter had both been discovered with their throats slashed.

"The man came into the kitchen of his house, up on the big hill by the railroad tracks, and found his wife. She was laying across the kitchen table, all the blood drained from her body on the floor. He ran through the house, thinking the killer might still be there. He found his daughter upstairs in bed with a kitchen knife still in her. She was still alive.

"Who did this? the father said.

"She wasn't able to communicate a name but she said, gardener. Gardener.

"Well, James Lampkin had been working for the family for almost a year. He worked in the yard. He worked in the garden. Worked in the fields. Did everything from planting roses in the front yard to planting corn in the back to fencing in all the property from east to west.

Having nothing else to go on except his dying daughter's last word, the father led the sheriff and a posse out to the fields, where James Lampkin was busy tilling the soil, getting ready to plant some peas, corn. Food for the family and maybe just a little leftover for James to take home to his family for his troubles. His troubles was just beginning though.

"Lampkin, the father said, where was you at this morning? Lampkin looked up at the group coming down on him and got scared.

"I ain't been nowhere but right here, sir, he said.

"The sheriff handcuffed him and led him away

from the premises. That group wanted to hang him right then and there. Picked out a tree and everything. The sheriff, though, he said, this man's coming with me. We're going to do this in town, out in the open where everybody can see. So they took him into town, gave him a thirty minute trial right there on the courthouse steps, pronounced him guilty of the murders of both of those two women, and hanged him from an oak tree in the middle of town.

"To hear my grandfather tell it, half the town was there to see it."

I had heard stories of people being lynched in the town for years. Art Patton's certainly hadn't been the first one. But even Art had never told a story quite like that. I almost felt sick to my stomach.

"They ever find out what really happened?" I asked.

Ted answered.

"Way the story goes, later, they discovered that an acquaintance of the family— a white man named Bob Gardner— killed them. Turned out there was a bunch of money and jewelry that went missing. James Lampkin never had a stick of it. None of our family ever saw it, that's for sure. They conveniently overlooked that part."

"Until Gardner was caught robbing somebody else in town," Hilda said. "When he finally got caught and went to trial a couple years later, all kinds of truth come pouring out. Money from half a dozen rich families in town. Jewelry enough to make Cleopatra blush. And guess who a great big bunch of it got traced back to."

Wow, I thought. Gardner. How had I never heard this story?

"I was telling your father about a guy named Art Patton, used to live around here a long time ago," I said. "He told a story that was pretty close to that."

Hilda seemed neither surprised nor impressed.

"Well, I'm sure it happened more than we want to know."

I agreed, but said that if Mister Patton had been talking about her great-grandfather, then it just went to prove that it was a small world.

"Goes to show that Patton's Landing is small, anyway," Ted said.

He had the last word on the subject, but, as I left their place, it was Art Patton's words that were left ringing in my ears.

Hanged man didn't have nothing to complain about. Nothing to complain about indeed.

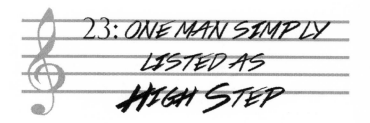

23: ONE MAN SIMPLY LISTED AS HIGH STEP

The Seed Store was right where it had always been, halfway between the turn off onto Patton's Landing Road and the entrance to Marion's Ferry, standing like a forgotten ghost from a different time, a different world. Its sign was almost unreadable—you could make out the name Delafield, if you already knew what it was— and about half of the windows had broken out. I was surprised to see that the other half hadn't been.

The front door was locked tight, and the wood around the door frame was still surprisingly good. I knew I could break out a few panes and pull myself through one of the windows, but I wanted to check out the rear entrance first. Walking around the back was like walking into a museum. Rusted out engines parts that looked too peculiar to have ever fit into automobiles. Wooden wagon wheels and iron tractor wheels. Plows and harnesses. Stacks of wooden boxes.

A large back room had been added onto the store at a later date, and, ironically, it was the more recent part that was starting to go bad. The double door was pulling from its hinges and beginning to fall in on itself. I could give it a push and gain entrance. I was only concerned that the entire back wall might go with it. The door was chained shut, so I scrounged up a crow bar and busted the chain. Broken free, the wall shuddered and sighed. I carefully pushed on the door and walked in.

The building had never seen electricity, so there were no light switches. There was enough light to see the kerosene lamps that lined the wall, and there was still enough day streaming through the windows that I wasn't worried about finding kerosene. I walked through the back room, which still smelled like coal. There were more of the wooden boxes, and I looked through several of them, thinking I might find some of the coal left behind. They all appeared to be empty except for rat droppings here and there.

I could see even better in the front part of the store, due to there being a row of large windows along the top on each side. It appeared that birds had nested along the ledges. Probably pigeons. Shards of glass littered the floor on each side where the glass had fallen in to give the birds— and who knew what else— access. The big stove stood squarely in the center, having waited a couple of generations for a light. It was warm in the building, but I wondered if it would work after all these years. There were two rocking chairs in front of it, and I stopped to imagine Art and his friend George sitting there, discussing the news of the day. One of the chairs seemed to be rocking back and forth on its own. I got a shiver all the way up to my neck.

The old cash register was still sitting on the front counter, the counter still stocked with tobacco and smoking supplies. The shelves, although covered in several layers of dust that were gold in the sunlight, looked like they were ready and waiting for customers. Some of the products had strange names. Coffee, foods, soaps, starches, household supplies. I couldn't be sure if some were meant for animal or human use.

Back in the back of the main room, I found the office, which consisted of a desk and chair, an Underwood typewriter, a stack of yellowing papers, and a row of boxes against the wall which seemed to have served as a filing system. I looked closer and found a record of customers and a sales ledger. Carrie Delafield's name appeared and reappeared, along with others from the Pattonia area. The Alexanders, the Turners, the Barlows. One man listed simply as High Step. And there, with four, five, six different entries, the name Art Patton.

I knew some of these were white customers, but most were likely colored. Not counting Art, there was no way to know one from another. No "w" or "c" written into the margins. But, from the looks of things, George Delafield had extended credit to one and all, when it was needed. Most, I could see, had paid back in full.

As is my usual practice, I moved past all of the other stacks of records and went all the way to the back. The ledger there was falling apart, its binding kept together only by years of spider webs. I took one of the other books and knocked it clean, or at least clean enough to pick it up. It fell apart in my hands, leaving only the papers inside.

The records from the years when the store had served as a mortuary.

I placed the papers inside of a folder and tucked it under my arm.

24: DYING OF INFLUENCE

The undertaker's records were a goldmine of information. They spanned the years from just after the Civil War until the turn of the century, and between them and the tombstones in Mount Violet, I was able to account for a good percentage of the people who had died in the Patton's Landing area.

Mount Violet, like all cemeteries at that time, was carefully segregated between the colored section and the white section. A notion that struck me as odd. It seemed that once we were in our graves, all things were pretty much equal. One set of bones no different from the other. Because Pattonia, during its heyday, operated largely on the backs of its colored population, that portion of the cemetery was much larger than the white portion. It lay at the east end of the grounds, two short rows of stones where the rest covered at least half an acre.

Several members of the Patton family were buried in the white end, as was Lovey Delafield, who arrived far ahead of her own mother. Many of the oldest headstones were unreadable, to stand there and gaze upon them, but Mrs. Collette in the office had suggested that I bring paper and a pencil and etch the stones.

"That way, you'll have something to bring back and look at," she said.

I was glad I did. One of the stones that was in the worst shape came alive beneath the pencil lead. A pair of hands held in prayer over the words "Gone Home October 10, 1872." No birth date listed. Beneath that, the name Jodora Conray. I almost cried.

I searched in vain for another member of her family. No Victor. No Wash. No Art. There were Conrays, white Conrays and colored Conrays, but no J.T. or Lucy or even Jed. The ones that were there all seemed to belong together, more mothers than fathers, children who had died either in childhood or soon after birth.

For the most part, the undertaker records lined up with the headstones, but there were a few names listed in the old book that couldn't be accounted for in Mount Violet. No doubt, people who came from other places and wished to be returned there. One such case was the guy who went by High Step. Dead on Christmas Day of 1912 and embalmed on the next. Reasons for death were mostly normal and mundane, except for the several notations of people dying of Influence. I momentarily wondered what kind of influence that might be before it dawned on me. Influenza. Normal and mundane.

Sarah Ellen and Kate Alexander were a mother and daughter, buried in the same casket. Others died of diphtheria. Smallpox. Falls from horses and tree branches. It seems like, for such a small place, there sure was a lot of dying.

One thing I didn't see was a little boy dead at the hands of somebody else, Art Patton or otherwise. I still had more missing pieces than found ones. Furthermore, some of the missing pieces weren't missing pieces. They weren't even pieces to begin with. At this point, I would have to wait and see if Art Patton himself could provide a few more clues as to which were which or how they might or might not fit together.

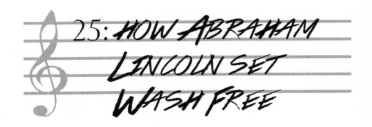

25: HOW ABRAHAM LINCOLN SET WASH FREE

"There were three rooms in my house, one after the other after the other. What they used to call a shotgun house. When you walked through the front door, you were in the sitting room. What my momma called the living room, although I did a good bit less living in that particular room than either of the others. There was a chair and a couch, and I remember nothing about where they came from. The house originally belonged to my mother Jodora, so whatever story there was there belonged to her, and she took it to the grave.

"My father's name was Victor, although it wasn't a name that fit him too well. There were no photographs of him in the house. This is mostly because there was only a couple of photographs ever made of my father, and in each, he's just a figure in the background, trying to get out of the frame or not even knowing he was in it. Which is fitting because that pretty much describes him in our life. If there ever had been a decent photograph of him, I doubt momma would've had it in the house.

"There are two photographs in the sitting room. One was of Jodora, my momma. In it, she's holding a small boy on her lap while a somewhat bigger boy stands over her. I was told as a child that the smaller boy was me. For many years, I had the mistaken belief that the person looming over the two of us was my father. In fact, it turned out that he was my older brother Washington. He was eight years older than me. Everybody called him Wash.

"The photograph was taken on a steamboat docked at Patton's Landing, just up the road there, a skip and a jump this side of the old general store. Best I can tell, it was sometime in the 1850s. Cotton season. Boats were coming to town once a week back then, sometimes an extra one on the weekends. I have no memory at all of the photo session, but I do remember hearing those big boats blow their horns when they pulled into the landing. You could hear them from one end of Pattonia to the other, and I imagine you could hear 'em all the way down here in Persimmon Grove.

"All the white folks for miles around— there wasn't a whole lot of white folks to tell the truth—

but they would throw down whatever they were doing and run to meet the boat. The colored men would load up the boats with cotton, timber, bricks. The white men would take the money for the last haul that had been sold down river, usually in Sabine Pass, sometimes Jasper.

"The women would be spending that very same money on clothing and material. Coffee. Salt and sugar. Whatever they had. It was just such a day that Lucy Conray stumbled into a photographer on a boat called the Kate who was making photographs of people as he went along. He struck up a conversation with Mrs. Lucy and asked if he could take a photograph of some of her workers.

"The niggers? she said. Why would you ever want to do such a thing?

"He told her that he had come from many miles away and had never seen such people. It was arranged that, the next time the Kate pulled into Patton Landing, Mrs. Lucy would be there with a representation of the farm workers. Momma Jodora, me and Wash were photographed because we were the least likely to give either the man or Mrs. Lucy trouble.

"The following year or so, Wash was sold off to a man passing through the area. Sold off because J.T. Conray thought he was trouble, and he was starting to get big. That meant big trouble, and Conray didn't want none of it.

"Now, the other photograph in the living room

was President Abraham Lincoln, and it looked like a painting to me, but momma always said it was a real photograph. That Abraham Lincoln picture had its own story to tell. A story my momma passed on to me.

"Everybody learned, in the years following the big war, that President Lincoln had set all the colored people in America free. Many stories were told about him, including one that he had come down South just before the war and had seen how we were all being treated, beaten and chained up like animals and with not much more clothing either.

"The story goes that he went to an auction where they were selling the negroes off for the highest price, and he started buying 'em up. None of the white folks knew who he was, but he had a big stack of bills, and they were all real eager to get some of it. At the end of the day, he loaded up two wagons full, mostly women and children but some menfolk too, and carted them all off. Said he had a big place up north that he could put them all to good use.

"Now some people swore it never really happened like that, and the ones that believed it couldn't get together on where he was. Maybe it was New Orleans or maybe it was Baton Rouge. Maybe even somewhere in Mississippi. Momma always came down on the side that it was a true story, just like the painting in our living room was a true picture. I think she had it in her mind that Wash might have been one of those that ended up going north with the

President. She said stranger things had happened.

"I would always say, stranger than a little old nigger from East Texas working for President Abraham Lincoln?

"He ain't working, Art, Momma would say. President Lincoln set all of them people free.

"I don't know if it's the truth, but I do know he set all of us free on a farm in the middle of Pattonia, so I guess anything is possible. I didn't bury Momma with the Lincoln picture, because it was the only thing in the house that reminded me of her. Everything else just reminded me that she wasn't around anymore."

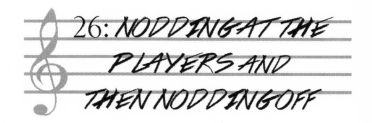

26: NODDING AT THE PLAYERS AND THEN NODDING OFF

Things were different at the Persimmon Grove fish fry. First of all, Art didn't show up until the sun had gone down and a fire had been built. It wasn't cold outside by any means, but it wasn't hot either, and so a fire was built so we could all see each other at least a little bit.

When he did show up, he was traveling with a rhythm section. A tall, lanky guy with a doghouse bass and a fat little man who made an old Ludwig bass drum with two tack head drums and a low boy cymbal sound like a million dollars. The two looked at each other the whole time, nodding their heads and smiling, Art playing across the top of them like a kid running through a funhouse. I couldn't be sure who was following who or who was chasing who.

For a long time, Art and his band played and the people danced. First only a few and then a few others. It was then that I discovered that if you walked out past the fire, into the shadows of the trees, a sizeable portion of the men were lined up and drinking alcohol out of jars, milk bottles, all sorts of containers. I decided I liked this side of the church a good deal better than the inside. They drank up enough courage to get their partners and dance, and those who had no partners danced alone next to the fire.

As the night wore on, the fire turned from a hot blue to a cool yellow, and the dancers slowly slinked away and either said their goodbyes and left for home or sat around under trees nodding at the players and then nodding off.

That was when the music turned itself down and Art began talking. He closed his eyes a good amount of the time, as if he was seeing the scenes play out in his mind as he spoke about them. I drew closer, so I could hear him better, but stayed close enough to the fire that I could see to write.

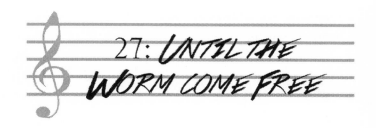

27: *UNTIL THE WORM COME FREE*

"I'll tell you what. When I inherited George Delafield's house in Pattonia, I didn't want anything to do with it. Not the house, not the carriage house, not even the outhouse. Zeus snuck by them on our way back home from the lawyer man in Nacogdoches, and I tried not to even look sideways.

"You could set your little ol' house sideways on its front porch, and still have room for the swing, Harmon said.

"What in hell am I going to do with a swing? I said.

"Well, you could sit yourself on it and wave at pretty white women when they come past, he said."

Not many people were paying close attention. It

seemed like he was talking straight to me. I made sure he knew I was paying attention. I was afraid he would put a stop to it all and disappear again.

"Harmon said, so who was that white lady a-waving at you anyway?

"Her name is Collette Edwards, I said. She had a man friend who got blowed up, trying to dynamite tree stumps a few years ago.

Must have made her crazy, waving at a colored man in broad daylight like that, he said.

"Must have."

I had noticed that one man had taken off with his woman and left two bottles of some kind or other unopened on one of the four tables that stretched across the area between the church and the little cemetery to the south. I was just thirsty enough to grab one when it didn't seem that anyone was watching.

"Harmon tried to talk me into selling enough of Delafield's possessions to pay for someone to move the house down the road to where I lived. I didn't have any idea if there were any possessions of value to sell off, and, anyway, I reminded him that there was already a house on my property and that the big saddlebag house wouldn't fit on it even if there wasn't.

"I'm fine just the way I am, I said, but we have two weeks before the bank comes in. Why don't you go live in the house for a spell. It's got a sight more room than the seed store, and it might even have a big old feather bed or two.

"Harmon said more room wasn't on his list of needs either. Things went back to normal. So normal that I had almost put the whole experience out of my mind. It was several days later that I was on my way down to the old dock which, even in good times, had never been anything more than a clearing where the steamboats could lay down a plank and was now just a good place to sit and fish. I had a cane pole and a bucket of worms and an afternoon to kill. A perfectly good afternoon to kill.

"I had caught a couple of small catfish and hadn't seen or heard anything else, except for birds and squirrels high over me in the pine trees.

"Catching anything?

Art leaned in toward his audience and brought up that low hillbilly voice. It almost seemed like an old friend turning up.

"I turned to find an older peckerwood in shirt sleeves and dress pants. He was swinging a hammer, but he didn't look much like a carpenter to me.

"Not much, I said. Not much.

"He come down the hill from the roadside, spraying gravel as he did. Scaring off the fish.

"Live around here? he said.

"I pointed west down the road and nodded. It was as much of an answer as I felt like divulging. He stopped no more than five feet from me, close enough that I could see the shine on his shoes. They weren't shoes for ambling around Pattonia. Let me say that. They definitely weren't Pattonia shoes.

"I'm posting legal notices, he said. The bank in Nacogdoches is taking over all of the old Delafield property out here.

"I pointed out Delafield's house, the chimney of which was barely visible through a field of pine saplings across the road. I considered mentioning the fact that it had been left to me but didn't particularly want to draw the conversation out any more than necessary.

"That's a part of the property, he said. It also includes the land back this way and here on this side of the roadway.

"He waved his hand around us.

"You mean you're taking the dock, I said.

"He scratched his head with the dull end of the hammer.

At this point, one of the guys who I thought was sleeping under one of the pine trees laughed really loud. Art repeated the line for him.

"The Delafields owned all of it, the man said. Owned it going back generations.

"I pulled up my line and splashed it against the surface of the water until the worm come free and swam away. I had plum lost all interest in fishing, yes sir."

28: DANDELION SOUP

"I had a dream one night, and, in the dream, the photograph they took that day on board the Kate came to life. Momma Jodora, me and Wash were back on the steamboat, and we were moving downstream. Now, I know you people know, in real life, the Angelina River is little more than spit and a raindrop in places. It was a little bigger back then, because they hadn't started damming it all up, but even then, it wasn't the kind of river you could imagine steamboats easily flying up and down.

"But in my dream, it had stretched out to flood level, blending into the trees on either side until it seemed the whole world was under water, but only by an inch or two.

"I don't know exactly who was piloting the boat downriver, but I had the good sense to know— maybe I should say I had the bad sense to think— that everything was under control, and we all were bound for someplace much better. Momma was talking, and I don't know what she was saying, but I woke with her voice still in my ears. I looked outside my bedroom window, halfway expecting water where the ground should be. It was still dark, but I could smell the day coming. I got out of bed and dressed while coffee warmed on the stove.

"By the time I walked up to the seed store, Harmon was warming up a bowl of dandelion soup and cutting up a potato from a sack we'd bought on the way out of town. A sack of potatoes cost a dollar and would last until they went bad if we cut them up enough. I looked at Harmon sitting there with no undershirt. He looked as hollow and fragile as his guitar propped against an empty crate in the corner.

"Going anywhere this week? I said.

"He pulled the soup from the stove and splashed a little into a saucer. He held it up to his mouth with both hands and quietly blew across it.

"Don't reckon so, he said. Might go down to Lufkin, see what's happening there.

"There was a colored cafe called Bunk's there that held dances on the weekends. It was also a well-known cat house. Den of prostitution. Just as likely the reason for Harmon's curiosity. As much as I had a taste for fun, dancing and alcohol, I had no great taste for women. Never had since the day I was born. Most days, I called that a satisfaction."

One of the women called out in response to that comment. I didn't hear what she said, but there was disappointment in her voice.

"I told Harmon, I'm thinking about going down to the house today.

"It's to Harmon's credit that he didn't ask questions.

"Sounds good, he said. After I finish breakfast.

I think I had me some of that dandelion soup. I always did like dandelion soup. After that, we walked east into the morning sun. It was buzzing with a cool chill that took some of the color out of everything. Along the way, we counted five posters, hammered into trees and posts, warning that the bank was on its way. The bank was on its way. The bank was on its way. We pulled down each and every goddamn one of those things, wadded them into baseballs and pitched them into the river."

29: THIS MULE NAMED ZEUS WAS NOW LEGALLY ZEUS PATTON

"Momma Jodora and my father were married after my father was purchased from a man who lived here in Persimmon Grove. Way I always heard it, momma met him at church and took a strong liking to him. So I guess it all happened right here. Mrs. Lucy knew my momma Jodora had a liking for him and wrangled old J.T. Conray into doing maybe the only good deed of his whole miserable goddamn life. They jumped the broomstick, and everything seemed happy enough until after the war. When we moved off the farm, Victor got what momma called an itchy foot. Couldn't stay in one place long. He wasn't around us much at all, and, when he was, he spent most of his time staring out the window and planning his next move.

"After Momma died, we didn't really see him anymore. He came to the funeral and said his goodbyes to momma and me both. Never heard another word from him, never knew where he went or what he was up to. Then, all of a sudden, my old mule Zeus showed up one day in 1915, 1916, hauling the same damn wagon he hauled me around in for the next several years. Only other time I ever inherited anything, and I didn't have clue one where he come from.

"Your name Artillery Conray? the man said.

"I told him no, it was Artillery Conray Patton. Most everybody called me Art Patton. He said it didn't seem likely there was anybody else in the vicinity with such a name, and this mule named Zeus was now legally Zeus Patton, property of Art.

"I still remember taking him to see George Delafield like it was yesterday morning. George was up on the roof of his general store, turning the sign around so it pointed back east, on account of having a new customer who lived down that way. First customer he'd had in two or three years, I'm pretty sure. General Store & Seed Store, the sign said. Then underneath that, smaller, Geo Delafield, Storekeeper. It was the finest sign in Patton Landing. You could see it for a good quarter mile.

"That's one fine looking animule you've got there, he said when he saw Zeus. Where'd ya find him?

"I said, He was just delivered to me

"You order him from Sears Roebuck?

"We sat out front of the store, and I went over everything that had just happened. George said he would wager that my long lost brother Wash had passed on and left me Zeus in his will. It was an idea that hadn't occurred to me, but it made sense. Wash probably would have called me Art Conray. He wouldn't have known to call me Art Patton.

"I decided it must be true. I wasn't sure I had much need for a mule, as it was just another hungry mouth to feed, but the idea that Wash had thought enough of me, all these years later, to leave me Zeus and the wagon made me strongly inclined to keep both of them."

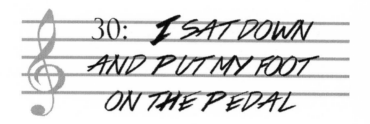

30: I SAT DOWN AND PUT MY FOOT ON THE PEDAL

"I had spent hours with George Delafield, playing, talking, eating eggs. He was always cooking eggs on the big stove there in the store. He traded in eggs, chickens. Said we couldn't turn them into money, so we had to eat them.

"Delafield was the only white man I had ever come across that didn't think he was better than a negro. He said it, and he acted it. He took in trade from negroes, ate their eggs just like he did the poor white folks who came into the store. This was a time when white folks would chain a negro boy to a tree and take turns shooting until there wasn't enough meat left for the chains to hold onto. I had seen that very thing happen with my own two eyes and so had he, so he was saying something to those kind of people just by talking to me.

"All the same, I had never stepped onto the porch of George's big house until me and Harmon walked up that day. That's right. I reached out and knocked on the door, and Harmon laughed at me.

"Think somebody's home? he said.

"Something in the back of my mind said there might be someone inside. Maybe some kinfolk of George's that I never knew about. Someone come to town expecting a warm welcome and didn't receive it or maybe come knowing George wasn't there anymore. I didn't want to surprise anybody. I didn't want anybody to surprise me.

"The banker had nailed one of his notices right to the front door, so I pulled it off and let it fall to the porch before I tried the knob. The house had big windows running all the way across the front, so the front room was well lit, the morning sun shining across the room and onto the wall. There were four big rooms in the house. The front room, which seemed bigger than my house just by itself, had a fireplace on the interior wall and furniture that reminded me of a hotel I'd walked by in town. The kitchen, right behind it, had a long table which would've held the entire populations of Patton Landing, Persimmon Grove and Marion's Ferry put together. I tried to picture George eating alone at one end of it.

"The bedroom was directly across from the

kitchen, and in front of it, a room that must have once belonged to their daughter Lovey. A small bed against one wall balanced by a sewing machine and a great big old organ, like what you would see in a church. The floorboards were starting to heave a little under the weight.

"Look at this damn thing, Harmon said.

"I put my finger on a key and pushed. Nothing.

"Harmon said, You have to pump on it, and he pointed at the foot pedals.

"Like driving an automobile, I said.

"I was pretty sure I would never get the chance to drive an automobile. I sat down on the dusty bench in front of it and put my foot on the pedal."

31: BLUE DICK

"There was another reason I was sure that Zeus had come from Wash. I had had experience with one other mule in my life, and that had been the old mule named Blue Dick back on the Conray farm. J.T. Conray had purchased him off the same man who had sold him Victor, and I don't know which of the two was the most trouble. Blue Dick was the kickingest mule anybody had ever seen.

"Wash was told to teach me how to plow with Blue Dick, on account that I was small and couldn't pick enough cotton to be of any satisfaction. Wash was a good bit older than me and bigger, and he knew how to handle him. I didn't know a damn thing about plowing or mules, but Wash convinced me that Blue

Dick couldn't kick while he was plowing, and that all I had to do was walk along behind with the single-tree and keep it in line.

"Smelling mule farts is the worst of it, he said.

"I still remembered the smell of mule farts when Zeus showed up a jillion years later, but I also remembered how Blue Dick got me in the hottest water I'd ever been in. I had only managed two or three rows when Blue Dick decided he was ready to call it a day. I hawed just like I'd seen done a thousand times, just like Wash showed me, but old Blue Dick wasn't listening. He was having none of it, as my momma used to say. He decided right then and there, we was going back to barn. He head back to that barn, and he was going right through the beans. Tore 'em all to hell. Then he went through the corn. Tore it to all get out. My very first day with the mule, and I got lashed within an inch of my life for it. Momma said I got it first from Victor and then from J.T. Conray himself, because he thought Victor was going soft on me. Which he wasn't.

"I still have marks on my shoulders from that experience. I swore I would never get close to another mule if I could help it. Of course, a week or so later, I was back out in the field with Blue Dick, only this time, J.T. had one of the hands with me, to keep me in line. Not old Blue Dick. Me. That was the year that things started getting tough on the farm for me, and I think Wash felt bad about it.

"Don't blame it on Blue Dick, he said. Mules are

just like people. They only treat you the way they're treated."

"After Wash got sold off, me and Blue Dick got to where we could tolerate each other okay. I think we both missed Wash the same. Blue Dick hung around the farm pretty much longer than anybody else. By the time the last of us had moved off, he was old and infirm. Couldn't half see. Couldn't hardly carry himself around, much less anything else. One of the men— maybe Victor— took him down to the pond and shot him, buried him where the ground was a little softer, so the buzzards couldn't get at him."

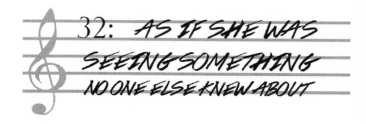

32: AS IF SHE WAS SEEING SOMETHING NO ONE ELSE KNEW ABOUT

"Behind the house, George had built a carriage house. It looked newer than the main house, mostly because its paint job was a couple of shades whiter. The carriage was still parked inside and in pretty decent shape. Zeus could've pulled it just fine, but it was bigger and fancier than what I was used to. There had been a barn, but it had fallen in and wasn't of much use to anybody except for scrap lumber. The wood line had moved in and grown up around it, making the top half the only part that was visible. Besides that, there was the outhouse. I didn't feel any call to check that out.

"This all belongs to you, Art, Harmon said. We were looking around at the tables full of knick-knacks and figurines in the main room. What was I going to do with a bunch of knick-knacks and figurines. You could tell George had lived out the final years of his life in his wife's home. He'd likely never moved anything after she passed.

"Did Lovey live here with them? Harmon said.

"Long time ago, I said. She died real young.

"Of course, Harmon knew that. Knew just how she died. Had heard from George's own lips how she had fallen through ice on the river after a late January freeze. How she had been pulled to safety by a cousin but had come down with sickness and died three days later. How she had walked out into the backyard on the evening of that third day and fell over dead in the snow. Still, saying that much kept either of us from having to acknowledge anything more.

"There was a photograph on a table in Lovey's bedroom. In it, Carrie, dressed in black and with a veil covering the greater part of her face, held her dead daughter in her arms and looked blankly into the camera. Lovey, in white, gazed off into the distance as if she was seeing something no one else knew about. The stamp on the bottom showed that it was made by the same photographer who had taken the one of me, Momma and Wash, but you could tell it wasn't on the boat. The seed store was cleaner, neater, but identifiable, a reminder that George had also served as the local undertaker. He quit the undertaking after that.

"It gave me the shivers, just looking at that

picture. And now, everybody in both photographs— the one with Carrie and Lovey Delafield and the one with us— was as dead as little Lovey. All except for me.

"I didn't mention my thoughts or the photograph. I said I was ready to go back to the store, and we were on our way when Harmon stopped.

"Wait right here, Art, he said. I believe I'm gonna go find that shithouse.

"I sat on the porch in the swing and tried not to think about the photograph inside the house. Of course, the more I tried, the harder it got. You know how that is. I was angry at myself for not getting George buried at Mount Violet. I was angry at myself. He should have been buried next to Carrie and Lovey. He should have been buried with the photograph. I was sitting there, rocking back and forth and thinking on all of these matters when my thoughts were interrupted, again by Harmon. But this time he sounded far away."

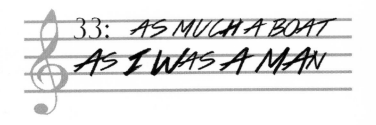

33: AS MUCH A BOAT AS I WAS A MAN

"Art, you gotta come see this. Art. You gotta. Come see it.

"I walked down the trampled path in the direction of Harmon's voice, smelling the outhouse before I could see it.

"I don't want to see no goddamn shithouse, I said.

"I didn't care if it had padded seats that tickled your ass and confederate money to wipe with.

"All of a sudden, Harmon appeared on the path ahead of me. He looked like the time he found a bottle of gin wrapped in a copy of the newspaper announcing Lincoln's assassination. Before he found out it was a worthless reproduction that they churned out like sausages.

"He said, This ain't no shithouse I'm looking at, Art.

"I walked past the building, which, I have to admit, looked nicer than most shithouses I've laid eyes on, around a curve and looked down in a ravine that broke off the river and snaked back toward the woods. I shook my head and laughed.

There in the ravine, dry docked and wasting away from neglect stood a steamboat. The name Camargo in a fading blue against the white. It seemed both proud and embarrassed at the same time. The boat was small, the only kind that could easily navigate this far upriver, but it had a deck. A sidewheeler, the wheel I could see was bleeding red into the ground like a dying soldier, but the bones of it looked sturdy. The wheel was about all that did.

"You could sell this thing, Harmon said.

"He took a calculated leap and landed on the boat's stern, which greeted him with a groan but held firm.

"Or maybe set sail."

"If that ain't exactly what I've been needing all my life, I said. A goddamn steamboat.

"I kicked a rock and watched it dance across the deck and come to rest not two feet away from Harmon. He just smiled at it.

"So what you think?

"I looked it over from stem to stern and back again.

"I told him, I might sell it for kindling wood.

"The hull had rotted clean through on the port side, which was causing it to list at an angle. Still, it as much a boat as I was a man. I wasn't seeing perfection in my shaving mirror, I damn sure wasn't expecting it anywhere else. And my carpentry skills were still good enough, I knew I could patch that old boat up a lot easier than I could patch myself.

"I left the boat there, but I couldn't walk away from thinking about it. In bed that night, my mind went back to the Kate. Wash was there. Momma Jodora. Mostly, that feeling of being so close to a real freedom. When the boat tied up at dock, the ropes didn't burn or bind. Soon enough, they would fall away, and the Kate would be off again, stopping when and where she wanted to.

"The feelings of a young boy were still there inside the man. You know what I mean? You know what I mean. I hadn't been my own person all those years ago. You may not know what that's like. But now, I called myself free. Free. And the legal owner of a steamboat."

34: A COLORED MAN LOSES HIS TEMPER, HE'S GOT A LOT TO LOSE FOR SURE

"I checked out the boiler and the engine on the old steamboat. They had rusted but still looked to be in fairly decent shape. Unfortunately, I knew we wouldn't be able to fire up the boiler and check them out for real until we could get the Camargo into the water. And we had to fix up the hull before we could do that. It was a flat bottom boat, made to skim along in shallow water when necessary, and the entire section that had to be replaced was on the bottom, beneath the water line. The entire left side of the boat was sitting off the ground, which meant we only had to crawl beneath it and lie on our backs to do the work. I put a crow bar in Harmon's hand and sent him up to the barn to pull enough wood away to patch things up.

"Meanwhile, I checked out the hull and cut everything that needed to be replaced with an old hand saw I'd found behind the carriage house. I was an hour or so deep into my work, laid out under the boat and somewhere else entirely in my mind, when I heard someone coming back down the path. I could tell right away it wasn't Harmon's lope. I hoped, whoever it was, that they were looking for the outhouse. I would leave them to their business if they would leave me to mine.

"What in the devil is that?"

"I pulled myself out from under the hull and sat up, the saw still in my hand. I recognized that goddamn banker's voice before I got an eye on him.

"It's the Lady Camargo," I said. I pointed in the direction of the name, painted along the deck. The sign didn't say Lady Camargo. Only said Camargo. I had already decided to add the lady part. I liked the way it rolled off my tongue. Lady Camargo.

"Banker man looked it over from stem to stern and whistled.

"I know at least a man or two would probably pay you a penny or two for it, he said.

"I shook my head.

"Don't reckon I aim to sell it.

"That banker man, he took off his hat and fanned himself with it, like the mere thought of a negro with a steamboat was about as much as he could take.

"Pray tell what are you think you're gonna do with a damn thing like that? he said.

"I stood up and dusted myself off.

"I guess you're wondering, what's a nigger doing, thinking he can drive a goddamn river boat, I said,

"He bowed all up.

"Now, Arthur, he said, you know that's not what I said. Now, Arthur.

"I wanted to say, motherfucker, I don't know who you're talking to. Ain't nobody here I know of named Arthur.

"I raised that hand saw until it was right between my line of sight and his. Shut one eye and drew it right down the middle of his body.

"I'm just about wondering what would happen if I tried to cut your goddamn head off, but that's not what I said either.

"Good lord, I could feel my heartbeat through my shirt. I think I tried to tell myself it was from working on the boat, but it was from either pure anger or it was from fear. I don't think I can tell you which it was to this very day. I know I wasn't afraid of the man. He looked soft, and he didn't have that hammer with him this time. No sir, he didn't have that hammer anymore.

"Still, I knew what could happen from losing my temper. A colored man loses his temper, he's got a lot to lose for sure. I sunk back down onto the ground and pulled myself back under the Camargo, as much for protection as anything. I sat there with my eyes closed for a minute and finally heard him moving. I turned my head and watched for his feet. They moved away and not closer. Soon enough, they moved on out of my sight. After another minute or two, I got back to my work."

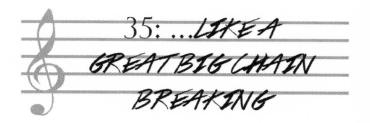

35: ...LIKE A GREAT BIG CHAIN BREAKING

"I figured I knew enough about steamboats to get along. I knew the boiler ran on coal, and I'd been lighting coal stoves long as I could remember. When the boiler got hot enough, it converted the water to steam and that's what ran the engine. I also knew that there was still a large supply of coal in the back of the seed store, because of the stove there and because the Delafields had sold coal by the pound for years and years. Every stove in Pattonia used coal back in those days, and so did the stoves here in Persimmon Grove and Marion's Ferry. Not to mention, so did half the boats that came up the river.

"The Delafields always sold their coal for just a little bit cheaper than the places down river. Whatever it was going for in Sabine Pass or Jasper, they would have a little bit better deal. Whatever it was in Beaumont, it was bound to be a good bit cheaper. They probably made more money off coal than they ever did selling seed.

"George Delafield had said as much. When I asked why he still sat on so much of it later on, he said when the railroads started coming through east Texas, the Angelina River dried up like a bluebonnet in hell. Steamboats stopped coming upriver, and it started a chain. What it started was like a great big chain breaking. People started moving off from Pattonia. Seemed like from one month to the next, the market for coal just fell off.

"George told me, his only consolation is he got a lifetime supply of the stuff, sitting back behind the store. He said, I might start up a fire all year long. And I 'bout believe he did. Even when he died, there was still plenty left to power the Lady Camargo for as far as I figured she would go.

"So we were sitting there— maybe it was the next day— and we were talking, Harmon Little John and me, and Harmon said, where are you going?

I had done told him the story of the banker— of how I'd raised up the saw and threatened to cut his head plum off with it— and Harmon said that it explained why he'd marched past him looking all burnt up. I was already regretting that whole deal, because I just knew that man would be back and probably with some of his buddies. I had already been served notice that I had a limited time to either shit or get off the pot, and now I had even less.

"Where am I going? I said. You're coming with me.

"Up until that moment, I hadn't given any real thought to where we were going. To begin with, I would have been completely happy tied up at the old dock right there across from the Delafield house. The fishing was good, the scenery was good, with the oak and pine trees hanging out over the water and the wild flowers and tall grass soaking up their surroundings. I knew by then that that probably wasn't going to be one of my options. The banker would be back with his hammer and his papers, and he would use big words to either wrestle the boat away from me or me away from the boat.

"We have just a day or two left to patch up the boat, slide it into the water, and then load it up with as much of the things from the old house as we can get onto it, I said.

Harmon wiped his brow with the brim of his hat and put it back on his head.

"We best get back to work then, he said.

I want to say that's exactly what we did, with the wind at our backs, but we both knew it was something more threatening that was pushing at me.

36: GEORGE DELAFIELD

"George Delafield's grandfather Howard owned more slaves than the Conrays ever did, and two of his sons wound up inheriting them when How, as everybody knew him, died. George's father, William, the youngest of the three brothers, made it known to How that he didn't want a third of the property, slaves or no slaves. To hear him tell it after the war, he could never stomach the idea of owning human flesh and blood like it was cattle. But he also had a natural inclination toward business. So William gave away his portion of the Delafield plantation in exchange for the seed store. For a long time, it was the heart of the community. I don't think he ever regretted his decision for a minute.

"After the Civil War, the War of Northern Aggression as most of his people called it, William's two older brothers— Howard Junior and Theodore— held onto the farm until it was sufficiently run down that they couldn't get nearly what How had put into it. They paid a number of the coloreds to stick around and help, but as the years went by, the brothers wound up doing more and more of the work, even as the work became less and less regular. The railroads hurt them, but George said the brothers held on. Held on for way too long, telling everyone that good days would cycle back around. Ten years later, Howard Junior finally got tired of waiting and lit out for Houston. A few months later, Theodore slipped down on a wet terrace out behind their house and slowly bled to death. They found him two days later. What was left of him.

"Meanwhile, William did real good for himself. When son George came along, he took over. They both made a small fortune, and by the time things slowed down, William was gone and George was ready to slow down. George always said he had more money than Ben Gump and nobody but Carrie to spend it on. I never knew who the hell Ben Gump was, but every time I heard that man's name, they were talking about how rich he was, so I know George was doing alright for himself. He was doing alright.

"When George's wife Carrie died, not long after

William, George was as alone as I was. We began our slow race to see who which of us would be the last resident of Pattonia. He never did really close down the store.

"George had what was left of a deer stand on the backside of his store property. It sat a good fourteen or fifteen feet off the ground because George swore that anything lower, the deer could smell you and would go the opposite direction. There never was much to the stand, and all that was left at that point was the ladder. That was all I needed.

"I had once heard of a band of Indians moving a big boat from the Neches River to the Sabine by rolling it over land on a bunch of logs. Each time one rolled free at the back, they would haul it back around to the front. The ladder consisted of a pole George had cut at the saw mill down close to Marion's Ferry and a bunch of two by fours nailed about a foot and a half apart.

"It took me an hour to cut the pole down level with the ground and pry the steps from it. Then I cut it into two equal pieces. Way I saw it, if I could get the Camargo moving, it was bound to gather enough momentum to launch itself into the river. I only hoped it wouldn't undo my patchwork in the process.

"I got Zeus to help me pull the first post the half mile to the ravine, but he was about as useless as Harmon, so I managed the second one by myself, one foot at a time. By the time I had both of them rolled up to the side of the boat, I was whacked. I sat down on one of the logs and looked at Zeus. I've never heard a mule speak, never claimed to, but I swear Zeus looked at me with a look as clear as the voice of the donkey to Balaam in the Bible.

"You don't think so, huh, I said. Not today, huh?

"I figured I could get the boat out into the water, but, if I did, the day would be spent and I would have to leave her out there overnight. Sometimes it's better to hold off and leave something for tomorrow. Momma Jodora used to say that.

"Zeus must have thought I was crazy, sitting there laughing at him and then myself, but he was right. We would roll the Lady Camargo out for her first voyage in many years, but it wasn't going to be that day. Looking back, I would regret that decision, but I didn't know any better at the time."

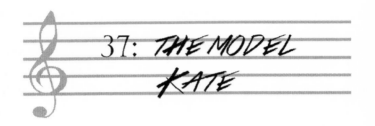

37: THE MODEL KATE

"The Conrays had a boy named Jed, or Little J.T. Jed was two years older than me, and he was bad news for both me and Wash, mostly because he was forever getting into trouble, and one of us usually paid for it. Usually me.

"J.T. had a model of the Kate steamboat sitting on a desk in his room in the big house. It had been given to him by the Kate's owner, and it was an exact replica, right down to the name painted on the side of its two decks. I never would have seen it, because I never once set foot in the big house, but I heard Jed talk about it. And Wash swore he had seen it one time when he was asked to carry a basket full of cloth from the big house back down to the quarters, for the women to use to make us winter clothes.

"Some time after the whole incident with Blue Dick, Jed got the question in his head, whether that model boat would float like a real one. Wash said that it wouldn't, said it was sure to sink like a rock, but Jed didn't believe him, and it made the question that much stronger. It was on a Sunday afternoon, after church, that Jed took the model down from his father's desk and carried it outdoors. That was the first and only time I ever laid eyes on it. That afternoon, Jed and his cousin from Nacogdoches took the model down to the river and let it loose. It floated all right, at least until a current got a hold of it and took off. The boys wound up chasing it clear out of Pattonia, finally getting enough ahead of it to grab it with a stick and fish it out of the water. The top deck was missing as was the paddle wheel. They spent hours diving down into the muddy river water and never found a trace of either.

"It would have been better if the damaged riverboat had never been returned to J.T. Conray's desk. I guess little boys don't think that way. J.T. Conray might not have noticed its absence for a long while, but he sure noticed it sitting there in such a pitiful shape, with its upper deck sliced off and the paddle wheel gone. J.T. called Jed to him and demanded an explanation.

"Boy, can you tell me what happened to my Kate?

"I can just imagine Jed's little lip stuck out and

quivering.

"It fell from your desk?

"Off my desk and into the river, Mister Conray said.

"And so, in order to save his own hide, Jed Conray accused me, who had never once set foot in the big house, of instigating the whole affair. Next day, I was called up to the house where I was shown the remnants of the little boat and asked to explain. In hind sight, I probably could have come up with a better response.

"Wash and me told Jed that it wasn't gonna float.

"I was beaten within an inch of my life with Jed standing not ten feet away from me, watching in silence. Beat me so bad I forgot all about the whipping I took for Blue Dick. Wash gained some satisfaction from watching Jed take a slighter but similar beating just moments later. I didn't get to hang around for that. I suppose old J.T. thought he was teaching his son some kind of lesson. Whatever the reason, it gave me no pleasure at all.

"Years later, when the Conrays picked up and moved away, we continued to live in our little house back in the quarter and never did move into the big house, even though it sat empty. Victor and momma never went inside, except to get some kind of supplies every once in a while. I asked momma one time, not too long after the Conrays picked up and left.

"I said, momma, why don't we move into the big house now?

"'Cause it ain't ours to move into, she said.

"That's all she had to say, far as I was concerned. Suited me fine. I never wanted to go back in that damned place anyway, and I never did. I don't rightly know whatever happened to the little Kate or the big one either, for that matter."

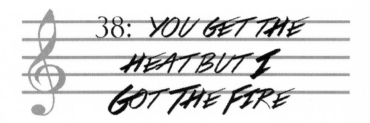

38: YOU GET THE HEAT BUT I GOT THE FIRE

Art took a break, handing his banjo to the drummer and disappearing into the dark. At first, I thought he had slipped away from me again. I walked up to the bass player, who was laid his bass down and was lighting a cigarette.

"Art gone for the night?"

He shook the match out and reached out to shake my hand.

"I sure hope not," he said.

I started to tell him how he had disappeared during his previous engagement at The Pepper Pot, then thought better of it.

"I think he just went to water the grass," the drummer said.

People had been sending jars of moonshine up to the band for the past hour, so there was now a circle of mostly empty jars that stretched across the ground in front of them. The drummer, who I learned was named Willie T, contemplated returning them to their owners, thinking, with any luck, they'd be refilled, but the bass player, Biscuit, thought they looked like stage lights.

"What in the hell good are stage lights that don't have lights in them?" said Willie, and then he looked at me. "Am I not right?"

I shrugged. Biscuit said he still liked them right where they were.

In a minute Art came walking out of the shadows, and Willie T took his place. I noticed almost immediately how much bigger Art looked when he was standing up. He had a presence about him that set him apart. Like there was something different about him, he knew it, and you'd better get to knowing it.

All the same, there weren't many people standing in the band's vicinity. Most were taking the break in music to say hello to someone they hadn't spoken to in a while or to continue conversations started earlier in the evening. I didn't want to miss my opportunity.

"I've never heard anybody play the way you do," I said.

Art sent Biscuit to get more drinks, saying he would watch all of the instruments until he got back.

"No two people play the same way," he said,

"because no two people feel it the same."

"Yeah, but we all get the blues," I said. I wanted him to know I wasn't just listening. I was thinking about what I was hearing.

"You right about that," he said. "But we all bring our own thing to it."

He reached over and picked up his banjo. Maybe it felt easier to talk holding it.

"You hear me talk about building a boat, taking off down river, what comes up in your mind?"

I had to think about that for a minute.

"I guess just getting away from the pressure of life. Being my own man," I said. If I had had more time to think, I could have expounded, but I was fairly happy with my answer.

Art sat down on the seat that Willie T had been using.

"You know what it puts in my mind?"

I didn't want to make any assumptions. I shook my head.

"I think about fixing up that beautiful boat, the Lady Camargo, and taking off from Pattonia, headed for the world."

Willie T had returned and was listening in.

"In other words," Art said, "you get the heat, but I got the fire."

"You get enough heat, you're bound to bust out into flames too," said Willie T.

Biscuit came back with full jars and an invitation for art to spend the night with one of the spinster ladies that lived between Persimmon Grove and Lufkin. Art told him to tell her thanks but no thanks.

"I might've said yes, once upon a time," he said.

"Shit, Art," Willie T said, "you ain't telling me you're too old."

"I ain't too old," Art said, "but I've done told you. I've been transfigured. I ain't that guy no more."

Although I hadn't seen anything to indicate that Art was a religious man, it seemed to me like something a preacher would say. That gave me the seed of an idea.

"I got a cousin named Eulalie Glover," I said. "She has a one hour radio show every Sunday morning in Nacogdoches. You ought to come up and play this week. She's always looking for good music."

"What kind of show does she do?" Art said. He looked interested.

"It's called the Glover Family Gospel Hour with Eulalie Glover," I said, "but it's more than just gospel. She talks to people in the community and other things too."

Biscuit laughed nervously.

"I don't know," he said. "We don't really do gospel shit."

I said I thought the music they played was as true as any hymn I had ever heard.

"And ain't that what gospel is all about?"

I wrote down the information on the back of a 1956 Standard Oil map that Willie T produced and let them get ready for one last set of tunes. If I hadn't had one and a half jars of drink in me, I probably never would have had the nerve to make such an offer to them. And if I hadn't kept on drinking, I might have realized my mistake a little sooner.

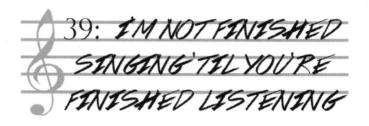

39: I'M NOT FINISHED SINGING 'TIL YOU'RE FINISHED LISTENING

"That fire looks like it's starting to die out. You build a fire, seems like there's always something working against it. The wind. Rain. Mother time. It's a fight to keep it alive. Well, we're here to hand down a whole other kind of fire. It ain't some new kind of fire I'm talking about. What I'm talking about is an old kind. A fire that's still burning on generation after generation.

"We've been playing our music and telling stories, bringing the fire, all the way across the south. I pretty much been all around the world, and I come back home because I knew it was time to bring it back. I sailed into Charleston, South Carolina about a year, a year and a half ago, I guess. And you know, people, it dawned on me that I was sailing in just like my people must have come sailing in two, three hundred years ago. But I come back and did it, I was a free man. And that gave me a weight. That freedom come with a burden. And here's what I knew I had to do. I had to pass it on. Not the burden, I had to pass on that freedom.

"Now we played our way home. Statesboro. Swainsboro, Macon. We met up with other folks. Folks like The 5 Royales. Lowman Pauling. Man alive, that boy's got the fire inside. I couldn't even get close to him. I'm not lying to you. Not even close. We played with him in Tuskegee, Montgomery, Mobile, Hattiesburg. Said goodbye in New Orleans, where this old music stick was born a long time ago. Full circle. And now, we're back here."

The crowd applauded at this point, and I was surprised how many were still there, off in the darkness but still awake and listening. Art and his band played a song called "Say It," and it went so well, they did it over again. (Later, I was to discover that this was a 5 Royales tune; were they as good as Art claimed? Almost.) They followed that with a harrowing version of Texas Alexander's "Polo Blues," the song Mister Alexander wrote about murdering his wife. Before he murdered his wife.

The fellows in the shadows were getting more juiced up with every song, their reactions more and more boisterous. By this point, they were no longer watching the same show I was. One of them stepped out of the cover, looking like a lost cowboy against the fire.

"I don't give a good goddamn about all this rain in Spain and South Carolina shit," he said. "I just wanna know, are we gonna hear what happened with that damn riverboat you was talking about."

If not, he was ready to pony up and ride away.

"And I ain't talking about no goddamn toy neither," he added.

Art never missed a beat, although Willie T looked like he was thrown off just a little.

"Don't you worry, my friend, " Art said, "I'm not finished singing 'til you're finished listening."

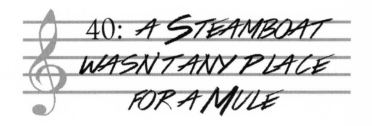

40: A STEAMBOAT WASN'T ANY PLACE FOR A MULE

"We got the Lady Camargo, with its new name emblazoned along the side, into the water. It wasn't easy. I ended up pulling the engine out and taking both wheels off to do it. Back in the river, it was easy enough to roll the two repainted wheels into the water, then bolt them back into place. Each wheel had twelve paddles, not big as paddlewheels go, but plenty to churn up a little action. I even took the time to reinforce that part of the boat with wood from the carriage house, just to be safe. Putting the engine back in proved to be more time consuming, if not more difficult, just because I had to clean it up and reassemble it before I could put it back in place.

"I had been a carpenter for years, though, having

learned from an old man over on Burgess Hill, in that area. We built just about every building standing in the Burgess Hill area, and I'll bet every one of 'em is still there today.

"So we got the boat safely into the water, and she appeared to be holding up. No leaks, no problems. I sent Harmon up to the house. Said get Zeus, get that big old carriage out from under the carriage house and start loading it up. Just get it and start loading it up.

"Harmon said, what you want me to put in it, Art?

"I said, anything that ain't nailed down. If this is gonna be home, we're gonna need beds, we're gonna need tables. Whatever George don't have no more need for, we do.

"He took off for the house, but then he stopped and said, books? Because George and Missus Carrie had themselves a whole heap of books. Books on business, on law, books full of stories from all over the place.

"All the books you can load up, I said.

"Harmon made three whole trips back and forth while I was getting the boat ready to set sail. The boat was as big as George's house, and it would hold as much of it as we could get onto it. Harmon come with the big bed. He come with Lovey's bad. He brung that long son of a bitch kitchen table, hanging off out the back of the carriage and him running along behind it, keeping everything stable.

"When I got through with my work, I would start on the furniture. Putting the beds back together. Finding places for everything. Harmon even took the curtains down and brought them, and I was putting them back up on the other end. Nailing in curtain hangers.

"Somewhere along the way, it occurred to me that we needed to test out the calliope up on the upper deck. I didn't have no idea in the world how to go about that, so I waited for Harmon. Him being the musical type and all. Back then, I didn't know how to tell a musical note from a bank note. Can you believe it?

"Well, we got to pushing and pulling on that calliope. Harmon called it a steam trumpet. We knew it was tied into the steam engine. That much we could see. And when Harmon would work the keys— which looked like any old organ, far as I could see— a big puff of steam would come out of it. But no music.

"Harmon said, maybe we need to prime it

"I was thinking, it wasn't no pump, but he said, yes, it was a pump organ, so maybe we need to prime it. So we primed it, run a little oil and then some water down in it. It blowed the oil right back out like you were pouring castor oil down a baby's throat. The steam trumpet was done for.

Harmon seemed to take the news personal. Got all down in the mouth. That's when I got the notion to bring that big ass organ down from the house, set it up on the boat. It might not be as loud as the steam organ, but I said I bet it could be heard.

"You know how goddamn heavy that thing's gonna be? he said.

"So I told him I'd go back up there and help him drag it to the boat. And that's what I did. It just about killed both us, just getting it out the back and onto the carriage. I tell you what. I don't know how in the world they ever got that damn organ in that house. Must have been, they just built the house up around it. We busted out the back door frame, which pissed off the bank people to no end.

"The bank people had shown up by then, nosing around and taking photographs with a great big camera. Asking questions they had no business asking. What was we gonna do with all that stuff. What did we need with a kitchen table like that. Did we really figure on playing that organ?

"All that stuff was mine. Given to me by Mister George Delafield.

"I would have killed my fool self getting that organ out of there and away from those men. And I like to have done it. But we got that organ on the Lady Camargo, and I put together a lift that raised her right up on top of that upper deck. Built a foundation that nestled her right up against the rail. She looked miles better up there than sitting in that dark bedroom, about to go through the floor.

"We were getting real close to pulling up anchor. We needed to go back and make one more pass through the house, make sure there wasn't anything else that might come in handy. I also had the final task of leaving Zeus where he could be taken care of properly. I wasn't looking forward to saying goodbye to that old mule, but I knew a steamboat wasn't any place for a mule.

"I remembered how Blue Dick had been taken out back and shot when we moved off the Conray farm, all those years ago. I didn't want Zeus to come to any such end. He might have been getting on up in years, but we couldn't have asked for more from that mule. He had pulled a whole houseful of stuff down to the boat, and he wasn't even getting to come aboard.

"However many years he had in him, I wanted to be sure he would live them in happiness. That's all I wanted for myself. How could I want less for him?

41: PROBATE BLUES IN NATURAL E

"We want to be sure you're not trying to get away with anything improper.

That's what I was told by one of several men from the bank who were walking around the house when I got back. One was inside, another was sniffing around the carriage house. One might have been down in the shithouse, because a third one appeared out of nowhere a few minutes later. I didn't know what to make of it.

"I have the legal ownership of everything in this house and on this property, with the exception of the buildings, I said. You don't see any buildings missing, do you?

"He brought me over to the man who had

shown up. A man who introduced himself as a probate attorney from Longview. I had no clue what probate meant, and I wasn't too sure about attorney either. I didn't ask.

"He said, It seems to me that there is some question pertaining to the boat.

"I said, I was told by my lawyer— see I wasn't too dumb to learn a thing or two; no sir, I was learning— Lester Massey told me that I was the legal owner of anything and everything on the Delafield property, not including the buildings. That means I'm the owner of the steamboat.

"The lawyer didn't seem to like the sound of that.

"Exactly what do you intend to do with the boat, if I may ask?

"I knew for a fact that banking son of a bitch, who I didn't see anywhere on the property at that moment, had gone running to this probate man and told him that I had come after him with a saw. I flat out knew it.

"I intend to take it as far from here I can, I said.

"He whispered something to one of the bankers. I had half a mind to whisper something to Harmon, just to show I was in the game.

"If you have plans to sleep on the boat, it then becomes a place of residence, the banker said. You are not allowed to take any place of residence on the property.

"I tried not to look as ticked off as I was.

"What if I only go fishing?

"The probate man shook his head.

"If you go fishing, are you sure you need two beds onboard the boat?

"Okay, I thought. This was reminding me of the word games me and George would play, time to time, when conversation got scarce at the seed store. Long as I didn't let myself get overheated, I felt like I could match wits and maybe even come out ahead. I didn't realize it at the time, but I was later to find out, that was part and parcel of being a probate man.

"Is the carriage mine to have?

"They both seemed eager to let me have that much.

"Say, what would happen if, somewhere down the road, I was to get sleepy and take a nap in it?

"Mister Patton, that's an entirely different matter, the probate man said. You and I both know it. For one, there's the matter of the bed set up on the steamboat.

"So, long as I don't make me a bed in the carriage, I can do whatever I want to do.

"It was the kind of smarty thing I used to say to Momma Jodora just to drive her crazy.

"I told him I wasn't one hundred percent sure Mister Massey would split the differences the same way, and that I would like for his input in the conversation before I said anything else.

"We all knew we were up against a time constraint. They were trying to work the clock against me, and I was doing my best to work it right back at

147

them. All the same, I did want to have Massey there in my corner. I could play the game a little, but he knew what probate meant. Knew all their little tricks. He seemed like a decent enough man.

We took a light load, partly just to get out of the house. I knew we could come back after bankers' hours and do whatever we needed to do. The other reason is, I wanted to take one last trip into town, drop in at Lester Massey's office and have a word with him and then stock up on a few supplies.

Far as I was concerned, the Lady Camargo was setting sail the next day, come hell or high water. I was ready for either one.

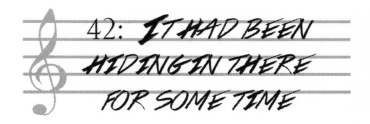

42: *IT HAD BEEN HIDING IN THERE FOR SOME TIME*

"I was prepared to push off early, hopefully leaving nothing but an empty spot in the river whenever the people from town returned. I knew bankers' hours, and they weren't mine. We would have made out alright too, except for Harmon deciding to stop by and get a box to hold his guitar. To be fair, it was I who had made the suggestion the day before, but we had left in too big a hurry to check them out then.

"George Delafield, you see, was a fair woodworker himself, and he specialized in pine boxes. He, of course, had started with his daddy, William, building them coffins for the bodies brought into the business, but he had expanded out from there. He made boxes for all kinds of things, right down to little bitty things no bigger than a matchbox.

"I saw that there was still a good assortment of them to be had, all stacked up against a wall behind the bedroom. I mentioned them to Harmon, and we decided to stop by and load up a few. He picked one out real quick for his guitar. It looked like George had likely made it with just such a thing in mind, as it had musical notes and shapes etched into the top of it.

I was looking through a couple of others, and already had one set aside when I heard Harmon let out a shriek like I'd never heard come out of him. Sounded like he'd dropped a heavy one on his toe. He immediately let made this sucking sound, like he was trying to get some wind into his lungs. When he did, he let out a racket even fiercer than the first one.

"Harmon, I said, what in the Sam Hill is wrong with you?

"Then I saw with my own two eyes, and I think I must have let out a holler all my own. There in that little box, with the lid thrown back and the morning light shining in, was a little dead baby boy. It had been hiding in there for some time, but you could still tell what it was easy enough.

"He sure does stink, Harmon said.

"That wasn't no dirty diaper, I can tell you. That's for sure. That stink was on account of him being all shut up in there for good spell and, naturally, on account of him being dead and all.

"Well, I suspect we better go on and close that

back up, I said. We don't want that box.

"We definitely didn't want that one. I was trying to think what we should do with it, and I was leaning toward hauling it down to Mount Violet and putting him away properly. Seemed like only the right thing to do. That's when I heard the front door edge open.

"My good god, what in heaven's name done happened up in here? It was the banker man from the day before. And right behind him come the very one I had threatened with the hand saw.

"Hold it right there, he said. You fellas ain't going nowhere."

43: *SOMETIMES IT DON'T MATTER IF NO ONE WAVES BACK*

And with that, Art and the boys piled all of their gear onto the back of a '48 Ford pickup with a wooden bed and said their goodbyes. The long lost cowboy was passed out in the back seat of his own car, his hat newly cratered for a souvenir. I watched Willie T take his drum set down, hoping for a moment to ask him about it. I had never seen a set like it. Sometime while I was doing this, Art made his getaway. He was there, and then he wasn't. Willie T and Biscuit waved and drove off in the direction of Dorr Creek.

I went home the long way that night, taking the detour through Patton's Landing to Marion's Ferry, then coming into Nacogdoches. I was halfway up

Laceyville Road, coming back into the colored end of town, when it occurred to me that this had to have been the road that Art and Harmon took when they passed the white lady on the porch. What was her name?

Almost all of the homes on Laceyville were big. Big and full of white people. Farmers, people who worked at the businesses downtown and the plants to its south. Most of the doors I still wouldn't have knocked on had I had a flat tire or car trouble. I could only imagine what it must have felt like coming through with a mule and wagon, thirty or forty years earlier.

I passed a couple of small, newly built homes with manicured lawns. Then, on the other side of the road, a two story Colonial style house. I had driven by it before surely, yet I couldn't remember ever noticing it. There were more like it in the area, and yet, the way its porch encircled it, as if it were protecting it and its inhabitants, made me feel like I was looking through Art Patton's eyes.

I remembered a nearly-forgotten incident from my early school years. Going to E.J. Campbell, the colored school, I didn't come into contact with many whites, adult or otherwise. The only place where it ever happened was downtown, going to movies at the Main Theater or walking along in front of the stores, all of which were owned and operated by white people. Most of them, we were instructed to never go into. In the movie theater, we had to sit in the balcony. In the department stores, we might be allowed to go in, but, like going in to the courthouse, you had to display the right attitude, and it helped if you had a white co-worker or friend with you. You were also expected to do your business and not tarry.

So this must have been either right before World War II ended or right after, because it was just about the time I started first grade. It was a Saturday, and I had been downtown with a couple of friends watching a matinee movie. I can't remember what it was. Maybe an East Side Kids movie or Lassie. After the movie was over, I was walking along and saw a handful of soldiers turn the corner and walk in my direction. That wasn't anything too unusual. The bus station was one block to the north, and a lot of discharged servicemen came up from Houston on their ways north and east, heading back home.

The thing that made this particular group stand out, at least to my young eyes, was its racial makeup. Four white guys and one negro. Walking along as if it were the most natural thing in the whole world. It drew my curiosity enough that I turned around and followed them for a block, stopping to watch them enter the most popular downtown sandwich shop.

This shop was high on the list of shops we were told to steer clear of. In fact, many a story was told of the shop owner calling the chief of police on some colored man who made the mistake of walking through its doors. I sat down on the curb, making sure I was well out of the path of any pedestrians, even though the street was fairly empty.

It only took two or three minutes for the colored soldier to walk back through the door. He walked a few yards in my direction and stopped, leaning against the front wall of the bank and checking his watch. He looked at me, and I smiled. I felt bad that I hadn't been able to warn him. I might have warned him against getting off the bus at all.

All of a sudden, a young white woman exited the sandwich shop— she looked like a student from the local college— and walked straight up to the colored soldier. She handed him a brown paper bag full of food. He fumbled through his pockets to pay her, but I saw her shake her head. She turned away and walked back into the shop. At my age, I didn't have a clue why, but it was quite plain that she was crying. There was so much food in the bag that the soldier shared one of the apples with me when he left.

I would see more scenes play out that way over time, but that was a first for me, and it stuck with me over the years. I often wondered about that soldier. Had he been in Normandy or in the Philippines, fighting for freedom? Did he still think about his stopover in our little town? Which did he think about first, the sandwich shop owner or the college girl? Did he remember that apple?

Looking at the big white house with the wrap-around porch and the picket fence, I slowed down and waved. Sometimes it don't matter if no one waves back.

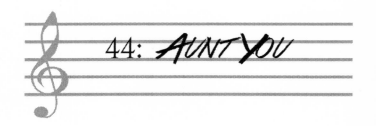

44: *AUNT YOU*

I spent most of that week trying to get all of my notes in some kind of order. Trying to make sense of the story that lay in front of me. I seesawed between absolutely knowing that there was no way Art would ever show up for Eulalie's radio show and absolutely believing that he would. The one thing I neglected to do was mention it to Eulalie herself.

Everybody in the family called her Aunt You— it was even spelled that way— even though she was only an aunt to four people, and none of them lived within a hundred miles. Aunt You was what she called sanctified, and although I wasn't sure just what that entailed, for some reason, it made me think she would get along with Art. Him being transfigured and all.

Aunt You also played a real mean organ. In fact, it was this talent which had got her kicked out of the Church of God, the church most of our family attended, if they attended at all. The Church of God didn't allow for any musical instruments. Aunt You, of course, fully expected them to make an exception in her case. I didn't go to church very often anymore, but I had been there to witness her attempt at insurrection in the Church of God at Saints Rest.

"I'll have you know I've played the organ, both a foot organ and an electrified organ, and a piano, but mostly the organ, in a Pentecostal church and an Adventist church. I've played in a Baptist church and an Anabaptist church. I've played in an Apostolic church, an evangelical Lutheran church. A Reformed Church. A Free Reformed church."

By this time, I think she was just making things up, but she got her point across. Aunt You was really good at doing that, and that's why she ended up with her own radio show. She said, from five a.m. until six a.m. on Sunday morning, the little radio station up on Tower Road was her church, and its membership included the whole holy race of mankind. That made hers the church that Jesus took a special interest in.

I wasn't real close to Aunt You, but she was one of my favorite family members. I listened to her program every once in a while, usually when I was still up from whatever I had been doing on the previous night. I liked how she always started off reading from the scripture, and then she would put it down and let her own heart take over. It usually got good about that point.

She also had an autoharp playing older sister named Earlina Harper that came up from Byspot, Texas every now and then. Aunt You liked to bring in musicians from the community. For color, as she put it. She didn't like them talking too much, but, as long as they didn't mind her playing along with them on her organ, she didn't care if they played the autoharp or the juice harp or what.

I had a feeling she was going to get a real kick out of playing along with Art's music stick.

45: ODA, ESTAR AND OMOR

Police Chief Battle was on a rampage that year, beefing up the law presence in the colored neighborhoods and generally making our lives a little more complicated than they already were. Whereas on the other side of town, he might have even been a help to me and my explorations, he was just another problem to work around for me.

Mostly, it meant I had to do as much of my work during daytime hours. That meant convincing my boss at the Gazette that, every time I walked out the door for the afternoon, I truly was working on something that would be print-worthy. To be fair, she was supportive, even going so far as to suggest that I go and speak with as many of the secondary people in the story as possible while waiting for Art to resurface.

I had a short list of names. Names Art had mentioned. Names other people had mentioned to Art. Names of people who were said to know everything that happened from Nacalina to Oil Springs. Both my boss and my momma knew of Oda Whitaker, although momma was fairly sure she had passed some time ago. It took half of an afternoon to find her place.

There's a way you can tell that country people are home, even when it appears that there's nobody within miles. The fact that I couldn't hear a dog bark or howl anywhere when I shut my car door made me wonder if momma wasn't right. I knocked on the door anyway. To my surprise, a young man answered. A few minutes later, I was sitting in a small kitchen with a glass of tea and an audience of Oda Whitaker herself. Oda who said she never forgot a name, as least as far as she could remember. Oda, who said her mother took the word "today" and lopped off the first and last letter to come up with her name. Who claimed to have a sister named Ester and a brother named Omor named after yesterday and tomorrow. People have lost the art of naming their children.

"Of course, I remember Art Patton," she said. "A couple of white men dropped him off with me and asked could I fix him up. Wasn't anything to fix that a bed and a good night sleep didn't do."

The boy walked in and picked a piece of bread

off the stove top.

"That and a plate or two of greens and sweet potatoes," he said.

Oda smiled at the boy, who must have been a grandson or maybe a great-grandson. Or maybe just another stray soul who she had picked up along the way.

"This here is Ephriam," she said. "He spent more time with Mister Patton than me or Ivory did. He's the one you should talk to."

Ephriam turned one of the kitchen chairs around backwards and sat in it. He didn't wait until he was finished eating to talk.

"What did he tell you? He tell you about being a hundred and nine years old? He tell you about traveling to South America and Africa? He tell you about his brother getting killed?"

I liked the way he got right to the point.

"Blue Dick," I said.

Oda was off and cleaning up leftovers from whatever meal they had just finished, but she couldn't help but overhear.

"He had a brother by the name of Blue Dick?"

Ephriam snorted so hard cornbread came out.

"Was a mule named Blue Dick, Big Momma. Kicked Art's brother in the head and killed him."

I waited until Oda had finished her work and moved on.

"He tell you what his brother's name was?"

Ephriam nodded.

161

TIM BRYANT

"Want some milk and cornbread?"

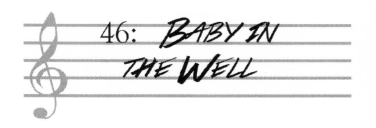

46: BABY IN THE WELL

"What if I told you I knew where the body of that little baby was."

I must have looked like he had pointed a gun at me and told me to reach for the sky.

"Art Patton's brother?"

Ephriam checked the room.

"Part of me don't think there is no baby, and part of me does" he said. "I don't know which part it is, but one of them parts wants to find out the truth."

He was whispering low— low enough that I could hear Oda Whitaker rummaging through something in the next room— but there wasn't any need to ask him to repeat himself.

Art had spent at least three days of his

recuperation sitting on the back porch of the house, playing his banjo and giving Ephriam a few lessons. He had also been going over stories. Lots of stories. Some I had heard before. Some I hadn't.

"According to Art, when his brother died, they carried the body up to the undertaker. His momma must have gone crazy, because everybody thought they was gonna end up burying her too. Art's daddy got word to Mister Delafield, the undertaker, just to hold on to the baby. He said Miss Jodora wasn't up to no funeral, and if they had it, it might end up being hers too. Art said that baby stayed at the undertaker for a long time, and then later, George Delafield must have carried it up to his house. Art said he figured the plan was to bury that baby with its momma when Miss Jodora died, but I guess the plan was forgotten or fell through.

"So then the baby got found again when Art and Harmon were moving things onto the Camargo," I said.

"That's right," he said.

I had the strong sense that Oda was hanging just around the corner and listening in. Not that I cared a whit.

"Well, Art Patton says that, after he and Harmon left, Sheriff McBride took the baby down to the old plantation and dropped it down the well. Said he didn't have no time or interest in giving no negro baby a proper burial."

I thought about what Bobby Lee Conray had said

to me.

"That could just be an old story," I said, "meant to keep people away."

Ephriam nodded.

"I know it."

We both stopped and nibbled on cornbread. It tasted good. Better than my own momma's. I wondered what she put in it.

"There's something else I need to tell you," Ephriam said."

He leaned in closer and spoke so low I had to strain to hear him.

"Part of me thinks there ain't no brother."

I didn't follow his line of thinking.

"Sometimes I think there was only two brothers, and Art Conray was killed by that dang mule. Blue Dick."

I didn't have a clue how to respond to this.

"Who is Art then?"

"I don't know," Ephriam said. "I haven't figured it out. But maybe it has something to do with this transfigure stuff that he talks about."

"You think he's a ghost?" I said.

I was trying to poke a little harmless fun at the boy, but he didn't take it that way.

"Something like that, I guess," he said. "Some transfigurized version of the boy maybe, I guess."

I tried to remember. Had I ever actually touched the man? He seemed more real than anybody I had ever come up against, but had I actually come up against him? Could I swear in a court of law that he wasn't some kind of ghost? I didn't think I believed in ghosts, but, then again, I didn't usually believe in 109-year old ex-slaves who looked half their age, running around with music sticks and wild stories either.

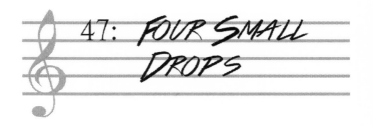

47: FOUR SMALL DROPS

I'll readily admit I had ulterior motives in getting Art Patton into the radio station. I had attended two of Aunt You's broadcasts within the past year, and had made myself useful by helping behind the glass. Mostly getting coffee and running errands for the station's morning manager whose job it was to make sure everything was transmitting as intended and that the local sponsors were all getting what they paid for.

I had also stuck around at the station manager's request one time when the show that followed Aunt You featured a western swing band from Fort Worth. The morning manager was a big fan of the band, and he had promised to reward the band with an acetate of the morning's performance. The station had a quarter-inch recorder and a cutting lathe that was set up to do such things, as long as everything was properly mic'd and all of the wires were plugged into the correct sockets.

"We're the only station between Houston and Shreveport with a cutting lathe," the manager said. "It craps out half the time, but we only got it in the first place because it's a pre-World War Two model, and our sister station in Lubbock got two new ones."

He showed me how it worked, cutting from the inside of the disc moving out. Then, I sat inside the control room, making sure the levels were staying within the proper parameters while the manager ran around the studio positioning instruments. The studio had one RCA mic in the dead center of the room, and it got a great sound. By the time the show started, I was relegated to the position of observer, watching as the lathe did its work and the band did theirs.

When I suggested that Art swing by the station for some live music, I had every intention of being there to record the proceedings. I was even prepared to purchase the disc. I knew acetate discs could be played on a regular record player, but I had no plans for any of that. I was going to take the recording to Houston. I would find the offices for Peacock Records, and Art would be a label mate with Big Mama Thornton and Gatemouth Brown. I believed enough in Art to believe enough in myself.

I got to the little studio on Tower Road about half an hour early. I knew the morning manager usually arrived in time to make coffee and get everything warmed up. Clean up any mess left behind by the Saturday night crew. Prepare for Aunt You and whoever she might be bringing with her that week.

I was concerned to see that the manager on duty was not the usual morning guy but a late night guy who was obviously still working on Saturday night time. He looked like a drunk who had wobbled by the station on his winding way home and decided to stop in and spin a few tunes while he was in the neighborhood.

I used it to my advantage.

"I'm assuming you were told about the recording session this morning."

The way he responded, I wondered if he really had been drinking.

"Yeah, sure, my man," he said. "We're ready for it."

The manager poured each of us a cup of coffee, pouring an extra one so hers would be cooled off how she liked it when Aunt You arrived. He took a bottle out of his pocket and splashed a little extra into his cup.

"Hair of the dog," he said. "Want some?"

I shook my head no.

He tipped the bottle at the slightest angle and let four small drops escape into the third cup.

"Just the way your aunt likes it," he said. "She says it relaxes her tongue."

I looked at the clock on the wall. There's nothing

as quiet as a radio station that's off the air. So quiet, it seemed like I could hear the manager's heart beating, but maybe it was mine. Aunt You was running late, and that wasn't like Aunt You.

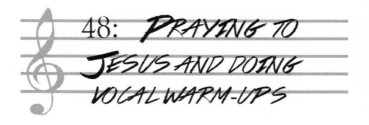

48: PRAYING TO JESUS AND DOING VOCAL WARM-UPS

Aunt You entered the studio like a field marshal late for battle. Calling for her coffee. Her music books. A chair. Where was the organ. She had already asked me to fetch two or three things before she recognized who she was talking to.

"I didn't know you was gonna be here this morning," she said. "But praise God that you are."

I knew there was no time but the present to tell her that she would be sharing this morning's gospel hour with a man who claimed to be a one hundred and nine year old ex-slave.

"Aunt You, I met a really good musician here, and I invited him to come in and join you for a few songs."

She looked at me over her glasses, which were perched halfway down her nose.

"Is he sanctified?"

I'm foolish enough to get myself into all kinds of crazy situations, but I'm decent enough to know that there are rules to getting myself out of them.

"No, ma'am, I don't think so, but he's transfigured."

She didn't look fazed. No Trans-who?

"Transfigured, huh?"

"Yes ma'am."

She looked around the room.

"Well, what does he play on and where is he? Is he invisible?"

The manager looked slightly more awake for the cup of coffee and sense of impending action and was busy getting the big microphone placed just right. It was a two sided mic, so he had Aunt You set up on one side of it and was preparing a place directly across from her for the guest. Made it look like a boxing match was about to take place.

Aunt You had two women with her, but neither was Aunt Earlina. They seemed to be working as her personal assistants, getting her Bible set out on the stand that was attached to her organ, getting her coffee where she could reach it but where it wouldn't fall and spill, fixing her hair up just right. As if anyone but the handful of people in the studio was going to see her. Meanwhile, Aunt You was praying to Jesus and doing vocal warm-ups.

"Something Pastor John Elmer taught me when I was just a girl," she said. "Don't none of y'all remember John Elmer, but he was around here for a long time. Everybody called him Stump."

The manager was setting volume levels from the booth and wanted to keep her talking. He didn't care what she was saying. Wasn't paying any attention to anything but the little meters on the console in front of him.

"Why did they call him Stump?" he said. "Was he missing an arm or something?"

His voice was coming out of a speaker right over her head, and Aunt You looked up at it whenever she would answer him, like she was answering God himself.

"No, sir, he wasn't missing no legs or anything. They just called him Stump."

She sat there quiet for a minute, looking over her Bible.

"I guess they just liked the way it sounded."

49: DON'T HIDE IT MIC IT

Art showed up five minutes before we went on-air, looking like a cross between a backwoods bluesman and a medicine man. He took Aunt You's hand and kissed it right on the knuckles, which seemed to suit her. He then pulled his music stick out of its case, which I took enough notice of to determine that it was not made of pine, and stood right smack dab on the "x" that had just been marked for him.

"Mister Patton," the manager said, "would you like to take off your overcoat?"

What he was doing was asking, in the best way he knew how, for Art to take it off. Art shook his head.

"It usually stays on."

The coat had colorful knick-knacks and things, coins and button-like medallions sewn into it, and they tended to jangle as he moved his arms and stomped around. Stopping that jangle before it was transmitted across the airwaves seemed to be of utmost concern. The manager looked at me with a can-you-talk-to-him expression. I shrugged.

"It's part of his sound," I said. "Don't hide it, mic it."

None of this seemed to make any difference at all to Aunt You. She was in her own little world, sitting at the organ and studying sheet music like she was reading a map before setting out on a trip. Which is probably pretty much the way she thought.

"Mister Art," she said, "do you know 'Let's Go Out To The Programs?'"

The Dixie Hummingbirds. On Peacock Records. My dad had a copy of it at home. She had probably given it to him last Christmas.

"No ma'am," he said, "I don't know that one."

She ran down a short list of titles, from "There's Going To Be A Fire" to "Just A Little While To Stay Here" to "Marvelous Name." They finally decided she would play whatever the spirit led her to play, followed by a few words of inspiration, then he would play three of his songs, and we would all play out with "This Little Light Of Mine." One of Aunt You's helpers pulled two tambourines from her purse and handed one to me.

"You know what to do with one of these?"

I assured her I was up to the task.

50: MARVELOUS NAME

Aunt You started the show with "Marvelous Name," which was my favorite of her usual repertoire. It was a signpost that the show was going in the roof-raiser category, and I was happy for it. Sometimes she would show up with her spirit out of joint, as she called it, and spend most of her time speechifying. She had even been known to take things out on the poor morning manager. I was there one time when she spent half an hour questioning him on where he had been the night before and whether he would go to Canaan Land if God sent a lightning bolt and burned the station down around them.

"I have no idea," he said. "Where exactly is Canaan?"

I still believe he was thinking of some bigger and better radio market close to Dallas or something. She spent the next half hour singing "To Canaan Land, I'm On My Way," even pulling the poor manager out into the studio and making him sing along. I didn't expect him to show up the following Sunday, but he did. He hadn't missed a day of work until this one.

"Marvelous Name" is an upbeat song, lots of rhythm, and Art clearly dug it. Sitting well off mic in his corner, he cradled his banjo, instinctively finding the groove as well as the key. Aunt You noticed him strumming along and came to a screeching halt. The manager and I both recoiled in horror.

"Ladies and gentlemen, I'm looking at a young man here in the studio," she said, "and he looks like he knows what I'm talking about this morning."

Art was watching his fingers make shapes on the frets. He might have thought Aunt You was talking about me, if he heard her at all.

"Mister Art Patton, I hear you've traveled all over God's wonderful earth. Is this true?"

Art looked up and nodded. The manager waved at him to move in closer to the mic.

"Yes ma'am."

"You've played your music on stages and even in dancehalls."

I cringed.

"That's right."

Aunt You was playing something real soft underneath the talking. It was beginning to sound like a funeral. I was hoping it wasn't going to be mine.

"Have you ever been called wonderful?"

"Yes ma'am, I expect I have."

"Have you ever been called marvelous?"

"Maybe so."

She stood up and looked around the room. She didn't need an audience. Far as she was concerned, the angelic host was her congregation, and she had their full attention.

"The bible says that the Lord on high, the seed of the woman, servant of the Father, He humbled Himself unto death, my servant, the branch. Can I get an amen?"

One of Aunt You's helpers supplied an amen and two or three claps on the tambourine, which was enough to start up a beat. Art plucked a couple of notes out of the air, and the manager let out a whoop which could be heard over the mic.

"The bible says He was the high priest, the living water. The mediator. The carpenter. Shilo. The Lion of Judah. The true vine. He was wonderful. He was marvelous."

The music was swelling, her voice riding over the top of it like she was riding a wave.

"Art Patton, are you all— of— these— things?"

She signaled her two companions, and one fell into line with the tambourine, the other clapping her hands and stomping her foot.

"Art Patton, I want to know. Are you these things? Are you the true vine. The true bread. The hidden manna. The Rose of Sharon. The dayspring. The bridegroom. The Son of Man. The Man of Sorrows."

He was standing. Stomping. Playing. Throwing his head back and digging it. I had never seen anything like it.

"Mister Art Patton, can— you— save— my— soul?"

The meters were pegging into the red, but it was a beautiful, rapturous noise. Art stepped up to the mic and let loose with a solo seemed to bounce off the walls and fill the studio up with static electricity. The hair was standing up on my arm, and I was starting to wonder if that lightning bolt was coming at long last. Half the room seemed to be saying no to Aunt You, the other half an emphatic hell yes.

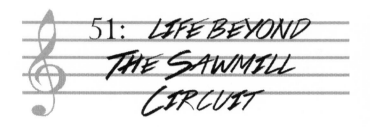

51: LIFE BEYOND THE SAWMILL CIRCUIT

"All I know, Miss Eulalie, is I used to be a pretty good carpenter."

With those words, Art launched into his portion of the broadcast.

"I was born a slave on a plantation in Pattonia. Property of J.T. and Lucille Conray. The president of the United States went to war to set me free. I put a broken boat into the river of the Angel, and she delivereth me."

"I didn't think about what I was doing. if I had, I never would have done it. I reached down, pushed the intercom button which piped my voice into the studio and leaned into the control room mic.

"Tell everybody how hard they tried to stop you,

Art."

"When he turned toward me, I felt for the first time that, instead of being inside the glass, the control room was on the outside. Art and Aunt You weren't outside the glass. They were on the inside. It was the only time I ever wanted to be in the studio itself. I turned around and grabbed the extra tambourine.

"I was friends with a man in Pattonia named George Demetrius Delafield. Now, George was a white man, but he was a good man and a good friend. Maybe the best friend I ever had. His family owned a plantation way back when Pattonia was a riverboat stop. But George came down on the side of the colored man. He didn't fight in the Civil War because he was just a boy like me when that come around, but he saw what was going down with his own two eyes, and he thought about things, and he knew.

"George died back in the 1920s. 1924, maybe it was. At that time, me and George Delafield was about the last two people living at Pattonia. And because we was friends, he give everything he had to me. I can still remember coming into Nacogdoches to speak with a lawyer here. Man by the name of Mister Lester Massey. So Mister Massey looks over his books and he says, Art, this is your lucky day. George Delafield has left you all of the possessions on his property. You get the house and everything in it. You get the carriage house and everything in it. You get the barn and everything in it. You get the outhouse and everything...

"Well, you get the point.

"Now, I don't think any of these lawyer men knew anything about the old riverboat that was on his property, but that was the one thing there that caught my eye. I'm telling you, it was looking a little rough. Like it might have taken on a little water if we'd try to set sail in it. But I was a carpenter, and I knew what to do to fix that boat up good as new. The Lady Camargo.

"Well, the banker people were getting everything that I didn't want, and they naturally were taking a pretty strong interest in whatever I was picking up. And that put it in my mind that I needed to take this boat and fill it up with as much of George's possessions as I could.

"That put a plan into my mind.

"I had me a friend. A young man by the name of Harmon Littlejohn. Lived down in Oak Ridge, just about halfway between Patton Landing and Marion's Ferry. I don't believe Oak Ridge is there at all anymore. But Harmon Littlejohn was a musician, played what we used to call the saw mill circuit. Back then, unless you was a carpenter or maybe a barber or something, that's just about the only good job a colored man could get. A saw mill job.

"Now I was already getting up there in age by 1920. You gotta keep in mind, I was born in the time of Lincoln. So I hatched up this plan to take all of George Delafield's possessions, run 'em down river to Sabine Pass and sell 'em. I knew I could get a pretty strong return on them. I'm talking good, white folk stuff. Furniture, silverware, enough books to stock up a library. You understand? So I had it in my mind that I was going to sell all of these things off and give the money to my friend Harmon Littlejohn, so he could go off and maybe see the world. At least see life beyond the saw mill circuit in east Texas.

"I never told Harmon that's what I was gonna do. I just decided to do it.

"First, though, we had to load up my new boat and get out of Pattonia. And that would prove to be more difficult than you might imagine. See, what me and Harmon Littlejohn didn't know was, George Delafield's father, a man named William Delafield, had been the undertaker man in Pattonia for many a day. While his slaves were all busy working his cotton and corn and peanuts, he was taking care of all the dead people. And somehow, for some reason, he had left one tiny little coffin in his home there in Pattonia. Yes ma'am, Miss Eulalie, one little bitty coffin with one little bitty baby boy was still up in that house.

"And guess who found it. I did.

"Well, I've found a whole lots of things in my life. Some of them was pretty okay. Some wasn't. But it ain't never a good thing when a colored man comes up with a dead body that he don't have no good explanation for. I can tell you that much right now. Before I knew it, the sheriff was there with his deputies. The bankermen were there. The lawyer men. Some guy walking around taking pictures of everything. And me and Harmon Littlejohn right smack dab in the middle of it all with no way to see our way out."

52: ONE GOOD EYE AND ONE GOOD MINUTE

"It was getting to be like a circus up in George Delafield's house. I doubt it had ever seen so many people. It was a pretty big house, but seemed like everybody was all crowded up in that one room. And finally, in come Lester Massey.

"Sheriff McBride offered to arrest both of us for trespassing or for public disturbance or anything else they could come up with. The bankers were pretty much all for it, and the probate man was too. Fortunately, one of the lawyers, who later became the district attorney in Nacogdoches, told them to hold their horses until he could see how things checked out with Massey, who he seemed to know and respect.

"A guy came by and took everybody's picture. Harmon and I both thought he was with the law, but they said they didn't know him. The sheriff thought he was from the paper, but the bankers knew the camera man from the paper, and it wasn't him either. Everybody was trying to figure out what to do about this renegade photographer when Lester Massey came wheeling into the front yard in his Roadster.

"He stopped in the yard to talk with one of the deputies, again on the porch to talk to the sheriff, and then right at the screen door to talk to his lawyer friend. By the time he made his way through the front room, Harmon and me were the last two people he hadn't spoken with.

"He said, there hasn't been this much excitement in Patton's Landing since the Laura hit a sandbar, and all the womenfolk had to be rescued in john boats.

"I told him I was sorry me and Harmon didn't meet up to those standards, but we could sure stand some rescuing. That was for sure. Well, it didn't take Lester long to drag out a certified copy of the last will and testament of George Demetrius Delafield, and he made sure to wave it under the nose of everyone he could. He looked around for one of George's boxes, and we told him which one to steer clear of. He grabbed the very one that Harmon had set aside for his guitar case and stepped up onto it. He was still not the tallest person in the room, but when he started to talk, he proved to be the loudest.

"The poor bankers must have wished they had

never opened their mouths when he was finished with them. He charged them with improper execution, misrepresentation, holding us under false pretenses and about half a dozen other things that I liked the sound of but didn't understand. Of course, the bankers started squealing like pigs, saying they were only following orders and that they were acting on behalf of the state of Texas, in any case, and certainly not themselves.

"Mister Massey raised the paper and pointed.

"Gentlemen, all it takes is one good eye and one good minute of reading to see that....

"He stopped to read aloud....

"Artillery Conray Patton is to be granted legal ownership of anything and everything of his choosing on the property, with the sole exception of the land itself, which shall be kept separate and turned over to the bank which holds the title.

"The bankers were looking at the sheriff like— is he going to arrest us?— and the sheriff was looking at Lester like— are you telling me I need to arrest these guys?— and me and Harmon were just looking at the front door and wondered when we were ever going to be sent on our way.

"There's still the matter of this poor little dead baby boy, said the one I'd threatened with the saw. Surely you're not going to let them just walk away without questioning them about that.

"It seemed like, with a single pronouncement, all of Massey's work had come undone. Such a racket rose up in the room that I thought the whole place might dissolve into fisticuffs. It was like an old western where the good guys and the bad guys are arguing over what to do with the outlaw, only I couldn't be sure who was good and who was bad, and neither me nor Harmon was the outlaw. It suddenly occurred to me, though, that this was how people like me ended up swinging from tree limbs.

"Just when I was about to lose all hope, Sheriff McBride stuck his head into the room and motioned for his boys to fall back. He then called on the bankers who looked like he had just ripped candy out of their hands. The room emptied out onto the front porch and then spilled out into the yard. Harmon and I tried to see what was going on through the big window, now shorn of curtains.

"Lester Massey came over and joined us, as perplexed as anybody.

"There's an old lady out there talking to the sheriff, he said. Either one of you have any idea who she is?

"I could see the sheriff's hat in the crowd, but I couldn't see who he was talking to. Harmon pushed his guitar case up next to the window, stepped up on it, then arched up on the heels of his feet.

"It's a white lady, he said.

"Maybe it's his wife? Massey asked.

"Harmon stretched a little more, then stepped down.

"Art, I do believe it's your white lady friend from

that big house with the picket fence."

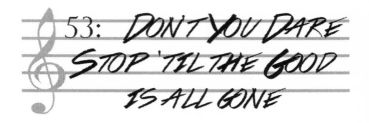

53: DON'T YOU DARE STOP 'TIL THE GOOD IS ALL GONE

Somewhere along the way, amid all the bankers and lawyers and sheriff's deputies, Aunt You got all beside herself and quit playing the organ altogether. I think I was the only one who noticed. All other eyes were on Art. Therein, I thought, lay the problem.

It wasn't that Aunt You took offense at Art's sordid tale. She just wasn't used to being upstaged on her own stage. Being conscious of the fact that she was blood kin, I knew I would have to live with the repercussions of the day. I worked my way over to her side of the room and then past her two friends, who weren't paying either me or Aunt You any mind at all.

"Aunt You," I said. "I need to pull on the reins?"

Meaning, do I need to get on the intercom and get this thing back under control.

She was sitting there with her eyes closed, and I wasn't entirely sure she had heard me, but I didn't want to talk any louder for fear I could be heard over the mic. I reached out and touched her shoulder. Had she died and gone to Canaan right there in the midst of battle? I wouldn't have put it past her to do something so dramatic. I tentatively pushed her, not hard enough that she would topple off of her bench if she was dead, but not so soft that she wouldn't feel it if she wasn't.

Her eyes snapped open and she glared at me.

"Don't you dare stop 'til the good is all gone."

Now, I'm pretty sure she was telling me I had best keep my hand off that intercom switch and let the man continue his tale, but it came across real loud and clear on the big RCA mic, almost like a shriek of ecstasy, and, of course, Art took it as instruction for himself.

"Yes, Lord," said the old lady with the tambourine. I fell back against the wall and gave my own tambourine a shake or two. I looked at the clock on the wall. Our regularly scheduled program had gone out the window.

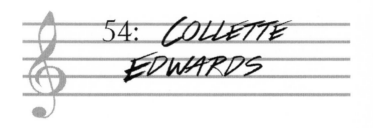

54: *COLLETTE EDWARDS*

"Somebody had obviously given Sheriff McBride what for, because when he come back into the room, it was like I was some kind of mustard gas bomb and it was his life's mission to clear everybody out before I went off.

"You stay right where you are, Patton, he said. Everybody else, outta here.

"He even tried to throw Harmon out, but I said there wasn't any reason for it. To tell you the truth, I was afraid for what he was gonna try to do to me, and I wanted Harmon there for at least a witness if not for protection. Know what I'm saying?

"Well, soon enough, everybody's out on the front yard. Some of them are getting out of Dodge. Getting out while the getting's good, as Momma Jodora used to say. And I'm standing there trying to figure out what the hell is going on. I just want to get on my boat and leave too. Pretty soon it's just me and the sheriff and Harmon standing there in that room, and it's so not a whole lot bigger than this studio right here, but it's been getting bigger by the minute. Like, every time somebody left the room, it got a little bigger. I thought about making a run for it, but that door looked like it was far off as the moon.

"All I wanna do is get on my boat and get out of here, I said. I was looking at Harmon, but we both knew who I was talking to. Back in that day, when the sheriff come around, you always made sure to let him know you was on your way out of his jurisdiction just as fast as your feet could take you. It never hurt, and sometimes it helped matters a great deal.

"Sheriff said, that can be arranged, but first, there's someone wants to have a word with you. You know a lady named Collette Edwards?

"I said no, sir, I didn't know of anyone by that name.

"He said, well, she sure seems to think she knows you.

"And then one of them deputies opened the front door, stepped to the side real gentlemanly, and in come Missus Collette Edwards, the old white lady who was always waving to me from the porch. I don't know if I had ever heard her name spoken. If I had, it hadn't stayed in my mind. But there she was, and up closer, she looked considerably older. She looked at me and probably thought something similar, but she smiled real big and come right up like we was old friends.

"Don't you look like Victor around the eyes, she said.

"I reached out and shook her hand. It wasn't the most promising introduction I'd ever heard, but, needless to say, I was intrigued.

"She gave me her name and I said mine, although it was plain that she already knew it.

"Mister Patton, she said, my family lawyer is somebody with whom I believe you are familiar. A Mister Lester Massey?

"I said yes, ma'am, I was very indebted to Mister Massey.

"Miss Edwards said, I have been wanting to have a word or two with you for quite some time now, and Mister Massey assured me that this might be my last fair chance to do so. He also told me what happened with the sheriff, so I knew it was high time for me to take a trip back out here. May we sit down for a few minutes?

"I said I had nothing against the idea, but that we hadn't left much furniture in the house. That it was all out on my boat.

"The Camargo? she said.

"Now I was sure enough catching an interest.

"May we go to the Camargo to talk? she said, and I said by all means."

55: WASH

"I remember your daddy, Victor, but it was your momma and your oldest brother Wash that I knew best, she said. You wouldn't remember me. There wasn't anything worth remembering to a little boy. Now your brother Wash was a good bit older than you. A good bit. Maybe eight years.

"But I was there when both of you were born. There was a colored nurse named Viola. I loved her to death. She spelled her name like the musical instrument— the viola— but she pronounced it Viola, like eye.

"I said I didn't have any memory of Viola, but it seemed I could recall Momma Jodora talking about her. We were sitting on the bow of the boat in two chairs from George's kitchen, and I may have been as happy as I had ever been. A fine boat she was, and I was happy to have Missus Edwards as my first guest onboard.

"The sun was sparkling on the water, and the breeze was blowing just enough to send ripples of light that broke against the side of the boat and disappeared. You could look straight down to the bottom, and you might even see a catfish or a group of guppies if you could hold your gaze long enough.

"Up on the shore, the sheriff's Model T was about thirty yards up the road and pulled to the side, and there was at least a dozen or so people just standing around and talking. Some of them were probably waiting to see if what happened after the old white lady left. Some might have wanted nothing more than to see the Camargo off on her voyage. All of them were trying to act like it was just something they always did on a nice morning in Pattonia.

"I worked for Lucy Conray, Missus Edwards said, almost twenty years, on and off. My brother Robert worked in their cotton pavilion, if you remember that. And it was through him I learned of Lucy Conray wanting help at the Big House. I know you must remember that Big House.

"I said I did, but I didn't remember going in it except maybe one or two times.

"Well, she said, I had worked afternoons in the hospital when we lived in Nacogdoches, doing little odd jobs and helping the nurses when they were shorthanded. But we were living on the other side of Dorr Creek by this time. Nacogdoches was too far. I was happy to find work with Lucy Conray, and she paid me. Almost the same as I'd been getting in town.

"You remember my brother Wash? I said. I was hoping she might be able to back up the stories I had heard. Maybe she would even add to them.

"Mister Patton, she said, I knew your brother very well. He was almost my undoing, or maybe I should say, I was almost his. That's a big part of what I want to tell you about.

"It seems that in the year before he was sold off into Louisiana, Wash and Collette had taken an attraction to each other.

"That was just something you didn't do, she said. We were caught talking out back of the Big House one afternoon, and I thought it was the end of my working there. Believe it or not, Miss Lucy gave me a talking to and let me go. I was fifteen years old. Wash must have been about the same, maybe a year younger.

"I told her I didn't have any recollection of that.

"No, you wouldn't, she said. It was kept hush hush. Later, it was your father Victor who found the two of us down behind the Quarters. He said it wasn't no place for a white girl to be and hauled me off by the ear. Two weeks later, Wash was gone for good.

"Collette Edwards looked sad. I tried to imagine her as a young girl, but she looked too sad for that.

"You don't owe me no apology for that, I said. It

was all I could come up with.

"We were young and foolish, and we spent our days like the wind, Mister Patton, she said, but I want you to know that I thought the world of your brother, and I missed him every day for many a year.

"I appreciated her words, but I wasn't sure what to do with them. They seemed like something for somebody else. I thanked her anyway and said I hoped she felt better. I had no hard feelings toward her.

"I told her it seemed like maybe we had shared some important things without me even knowing it, but that I didn't miss the days on the Conray farm one iota. Maybe that was the biggest difference between us.

"You may be right, she said. It's a funny thing. Most of my memories of that place don't bring me anything but pain and sadness, and yet I have to say, I do miss those days. I had a husband for thirty-five years, and he was a good man, but if I could relive any of my days, I would go back to those days at the Big House.

"What could I say to that? Wasn't anything to be said.

"You remember Jed and that model boat of Mister Conray's?

"She said she did— right down to me getting a whooping for it— and, for some damn reason, that made me happy.

"You remember old Blue Dick? I said.

"Can you remember that? she said back. You remember your other brother?"

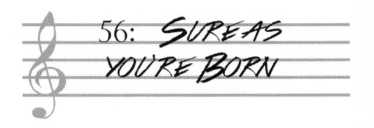

56: SURE AS YOU'RE BORN

"My other brother, I said. You mean Washington.

"She suddenly seemed to look older, as if some part of her life, a decent part of whatever was left of it, had just been sucked out of her.

"You had another brother who died when you were a baby. His name was Artillery.

"I thought surely she had things confused in her mind. She was old. Really old.

"Artillery, I said.

"That's right. They called him Art like you. She would say it's Artillery for his destructive power and Art for his creative power. You didn't even have a name. They didn't name negro babies back then like they do now. Sometimes a negro baby wouldn't have a name until he was walking and talking. Old enough to say it and recognize it when it was said.

"I didn't know how to proceed with my part of the conversation. I was almost positive that she had gotten her memories crossed up. Hell, for all I knew, maybe she had gone soft headed. I wanted to end the conversation and be on my way. But then, I didn't.

"What happened to Art?" I said. I said it real matter-of-factly, like I was asking about the weather report for the rest of the day. It seemed so disconnected from me, it was about the same.

"Miss Edwards said, Neither one of your parents ever got over that, I don't guess. They both took it in their own individual ways. Your momma, God bless her, tried to go on like nothing had happened. She said she had a vision— a dream, I suppose— and God had told her that you would be everything that that little boy was supposed to be. That's why she named you Art.

"But she named me Artillery, I said.

"No, she said. That's who you became. That's not who you were born to be.

"I remember noticing at this point that Harmon was standing five feet away from us. No longer making any attempt at looking occupied. Sheriff McBride was standing next to an oak tree just across the road. I wondered how much of this story he had heard. Did he believe it?

"You didn't answer my question, I said.

Her eyes looked dazed.

"What happened to my brother?

She glanced at Harmon and then back at me. Then at the Sheriff under the oak tree.

"Art got kicked by Blue Dick, she said.

Now I knew she was crazy.

"It was me got kicked by Blue Dick

"She stood up and grabbed at her purse.

"You were there, she said, true. He had you up on that mule, riding you around. If he had been on the mule with you, it never would have got him.

"I sat with your brother for two nights. We did everything we knew how to do. His head swelled up. He lost his sight. We prayed for God to heal him, and as things went on, we started to pray that he would take him. Your daddy wouldn't let Jodora see him. Your daddy came close to taking a pillow and ending it all a time or two. The way it all ended, I've often wondered if it would have been better.

"She held her hand out, and I shook it. There wasn't any reason for me not to. I don't remember thanking her. I might have or maybe not. As she stood on the starboard side of the Camargo, waiting for McBride to come over and help her back up the bank to safety, she spoke again.

"I still remember taking his little body down to William Delafield. Of course, I knew William and his wife too. Their son George. Good people, especially your friend George. A good man.

"She looked around the boat.

"He would be happy to see you get out of here. He would be even happier to know you were doing it on the Camargo.

"I asked her if she knew anything about the boat.

"Sometime before the war between the states, she said, a customer from somewhere down river had run up a pretty steep bill at the seed store and tried to pay it off by giving him two slaves, an old man and his wife. They were old, he said, but she could sew anything from coveralls to ball gowns, and he was as good at shoeing horses as anyone this side of the Red River.

"William told the man he didn't trade in people. Well, this fellow said, this is all I have of value that I can give you, so you either take them to settle my debt or be prepared to take the loss.

"William was prepared to take the loss, but that fellow's situation went from bad to worse, and pretty soon, he was reduced to selling off everything he had. William wound up buying the Camargo from them for a small price and calling it even. He took that old colored couple too, and paid them a wage for several years to help out around the store.

"I knew this story to be true, because I had heard it from George's mouth. The two old slaves that his father had given a job. I could even name them. Avery and Rachel Goodman. How can you forget a name like Avery Goodman. A very good man. But I didn't mention it. She left with Sheriff McBride, who told me I would be wise to put as much distance between myself and Nacogdoches County as I could.

"Not a single word about any of it was spoken between Harmon and me that day, and not for a number of days after. I did do some thinking on it though. When it all came down to it, I knew Collette Edwards was right. She wouldn't have waved at me from her front porch like she had. She wouldn't have waited all that time just to pass on a lie. What's more, I knew that that was my brother in that box back in George Delafield's bedroom. Sure as you're born, it was him."

57: *BIG FINISH*

Art:
This little light of mine
I'm gonna let it shine
This little light of mine
I'm gonna let it shine
This little light of mine
I'm gonna let it shine
Let it shine, let it shine, let it shine, shine, shine
Let it shine, let it shine shine shine

When I take my boat down river
I'm gonna let it shine
When I take my boat down river
I'm gonna let it shine

When I take my boat down river
I'm gonna let it shine
Let it shine, let it shine, let it shine, shine, shine
Let it shine, let it shine shine shine

Aunt You:
Jesus gave this light to me
I'm gonna let it shine
Jesus gave this light to me
I'm gonna let it shine
I once was blind, now I can see
I'm gonna let it shine
Let it shine, let it shine, let it shine, shine, shine
Let it shine, let it shine shine shine

AUNT YOU'S ORGAN SOLO

Aunt You:
Don't let Satan blow it out
I'm gonna let it shine
Don't let Satan blow it out
I'm gonna let it shine
Don't let Satan blow it out
I'm gonna let it shine
Let it shine, let it shine, let it shine, shine, shine
Let it shine, let it shine shine shine

Art:
All the way to Africa

I'm gonna let it shine
All the way to Africa
I'm gonna let it shine
All the way to South America
I'm gonna let it shine
Let it shine, let it shine, let it shine, shine, shine
Let it shine, let it shine shine shine

ART'S SOLO

Art and Aunt You:
Hide it under a bushel, no
I'm gonna let it shine
Ain't gonna let 'em hide it, no
I'm gonna let it shine
Hide it under a bushel, no
I'm gonna let it shine
Let it shine, let it shine, let it shine, shine, shine
Let it shine, let it shine shine shine

Aunt You:
On my way to Canaan land
I'm gonna let it shine
On my way to Canaan land
I'm gonna let it shine
I'm on my way to Canaan, Lord
I'm gonna let it shine
Let it shine, let it shine, let it shine, shine, shine
Let it shine, let it shine shine shine

CONSTELLATIONS

Art:
Hello Central
Please give me 209
Hello Central
Please give me 209
Hello Central
Please give me 209
Keep your hands off of it,
'cause it's mine, mine, mine
Let it shine, let it shine shine shine

ART'S SOLO 2

58: PEOPLE ON THE ROADSIDE

I used to be of the opinion that time was a constant, maybe the only constant. I no longer hold that belief. I've had weeks flash by without seeming to notice, and I've seen a day or two stretch out so long in front of me, I never thought they would end.

The next couple of days were like that.

Art had said more than once that he had been transfigurated, and I decided to find out everything I could about the word. The concept. What Art meant when he said it. The little library in downtown Nacogdoches wasn't welcoming to the colored residents, but I knew two or three different people in our community who had personal libraries that were just as useful. One was the superintendent of the colored school. One was a deacon in the Methodist Church.

Thinking that being transfigured seemed like some kind of religious thing, I went to Deacon Dupre first. Deacon Dupre said he thought it was a Catholic thing, but I was welcome to borrow his Encyclopedia on Major World Religions if I thought it might be of some help. Dr. Elias Hines from the high school said he was almost positive that Jesus himself had been transfigured, but he wasn't sure when or exactly how.

I was getting nowhere, both figuratively and literally, so I took a ride. It had been my habit for some time to take the family car out for a drive when I needed to get away and clear my head. Normally, I would stay within certain parameters, all on the south and east side of town. Lately, I had taken to driving south. Press Road or the one toward Woden. Watching people on the roadside.

Who was this man who called himself Artillery Conray Patton? The question had been on my mind since the night at The Pepper Pot. I had written page after page trying to work myself toward an answer. Some glimpse of truth. I dreamed about it at night. And then, after the Sunday morning radio broadcast, the question had shifted. It had become more unsettling. Instead of dreaming about it at night, I laid awake, going over and over it.

If I were to believe the story, Art Patton didn't know who Art Patton was. If that were the case, my story became more than a story. It was no longer a chance to tell readers something that would enrich their lives. It became an opportunity to tell Art something that would define his.

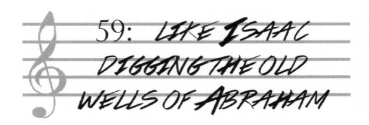

59: LIKE ISAAC DIGGING THE OLD WELLS OF ABRAHAM

"Like Isaac digging the old wells of Abraham," Ephriam said.

I didn't have any idea what he was talking about, but I agreed anyway.

"If Abraham dug up the ghost of a dead baby," I said.

We were back on what was left of the Conray plantation. I had found the old slave quarters easy enough, taking time to paint some kind of picture of how they had looked originally. Where there were now two, there had once been eight or ten, all pointing back in the direction of Billy Conray's place, which appeared to be empty. I showed Ephriam the area that I believed to have once been the pond, and then pointed out the general direction of the Big House.

Once he got a lay of the land, we grabbed shovels and set out to find some evidence of the wells. The old wells of Conray. The undergrowth made it hard to see the forest floor in most places, and I told him there was likely to be very little except maybe the foundation left from the house, and maybe even less of the wells.

As Ephriam swept across the area in front of him, already getting dark under the cover of pines, he called out to me.

"So old Blue Dick is buried somewhere right out in here."

I said yes, if the story was true. I went to work, pushing layer upon layer of brush away to reveal the damp earth below. The smell was strong. Life and death and rebirth all set free from their places in the cycle.

"You know the very first song you ever heard Art Patton sing?"

I thought for a minute but was surprised to find I couldn't name it.

"Probably a Lightnin' Hopkins," I said.

I could almost hear Ephriam grin. He was swinging his flat shovel, not so far off to the right of me that I couldn't hear it sweep and swipe against the ground. Suddenly, he started to singing in time.

You can't read, you can't write

CONSTELLATIONS

You can't get no supper tonight
You can't read, you can't write
You can't get no supper tonight

Had any young couple pulled up on the road at that moment, they would have thought they were hearing a ghost from a different time for sure. The hair stood up on my arm. It seemed to me that everything had been turned around. We were the ghosts, come back to a distant past to scare up our own ancestors. I was losing myself in just such a convoluted thought when Ephriam gave out a shout. Not a frightened shout necessarily, but an excited one. The song, as good as it was, was cut short.

"Found something," he said.

His shovel was sticking out a pile of red dirt about half a foot below the forest floor. Around the base of it, you could see the remnants of a stone foundation.

"Looks like someone's been digging here before," Ephriam said.

I stuck my shovel into it. It was sticky and clay-like and wouldn't shake off.

"I don't think so," I said, picking through the surrounding foliage like I was picking through bad food with a fork. "More likely it's just settled over time Might still be a natural spring underneath it."

I tossed a shovel full of hard dirt to one side, leaving everything in its path stained a blood red.

"Could be it's the wrong well," Ephriam said.

We both knew the story. How an older, smaller well had been abandoned and a bigger one built some distance away. Of course, there would be no way to tell which was which until we found both, and even then it might prove difficult. We decided that I should continue to look for signs of another one, while Ephriam dug around a little at this one. I grabbed my shovel and took off in what I believed to be the direction of the Big House. Stood to reason if they dug a new one, somebody would suggest that they do it closer to the house. The moon was just rising up out of that same direction, which would help me keep my bearings.

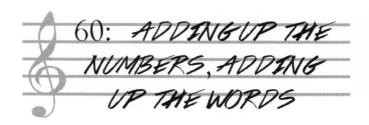

60: ADDING UP THE NUMBERS, ADDING UP THE WORDS

"So tell me something. It ever strike you that maybe this guy is Harmon Littlejohn," I said. "I mean, has he ever come out and said what happened to that guy?"

I had sat down more than once, adding up the numbers, adding up the words. It was something that had been moved from the back of my mind to the tip of my tongue, and I finally found someone to say it to.

"Harmon Littlejohn?"

I don't know if it was because we were so close to the river or what, but the dirt seemed to be getting looser as Ephriam went. Talking didn't even slow him down.

"Art pretty much admits that he was going down river to sell off all that stuff, right" said Paul. "From what I understand, he was going to give the money to Harmon. Did he ever say whether he did that?"

I wanted to defend Art's story, but it wasn't easy. I wanted to believe without having to actually reason any of it out. Kind of the way Aunt You did with the Lord.

"He told me the whole story one day while we were playing music on the back porch," Ephriam said.

If I'm being honest, I have to admit the thought made me a little jealous. Not so jealous that I didn't want to hear it, mind you. Maybe envious is a better word.

"See, that don't add up either," I said. "I thought Little John was the musician. Did he teach Art how to play or what?"

I could keep looking for a second well or I could join Ephriam and pick up speed. The hole he was in looked to be about six, maybe seven feet wide. Pretty big for a well. Big enough for both of us to stand at the bottom and sling a little dirt.

"Art learned how to play over in Africa, after Harmon Littlejohn was already dead and gone."

I jumped in with both feet.

61: MY NAME IS ANGEL

"We went down to Sabine Pass. Back then, I thought Sabine Pass was the end of the world. I didn't know there was anything else. We got down there okay. We made a stop in Lufkin, but two colored people on a riverboat by their selves was just too much for people to process. Everybody wanted to have a look. The boat wasn't enough. They wanted to take a good look at me and Harmon too. I don't know where they thought we'd sailed from, but I don't think it was Pattonia.

"We got to Jasper, and one old boy brought some beef jelly sandwiches, soda crackers and sorghum candy. He said we weren't far from Sabine Pass, and he was right. We made it there directly and pulled the Lady Camargo into port and tied up. It took us three or four days there in Sabine pass. I can't remember for sure. We took our first load in to sell. I left Harmon there guarding the ship, you know, and paid a boy that wasn't too much smaller than him to help me tote everything into town.

"I was aiming to sell at this first place I come to, and there was a long line of people waiting to sell their own wares or maybe buy somebody else's. I wasn't standing there more than an hour when this man comes out and looks at me. I look back, trying to make out whether he thought he knew me from somewhere. Or maybe he did, but I didn't recognize him.

"He took a long look at my merchandise— just a sample of everything we had stored up on that boat— and said, Mister, you ought to take what you got and go on down to this other place. He give me the number and name of the street. He said, my name is Angel. My uncle works there. Ask for him. I guarantee he'll give you a better price.

"I never did find out what that first place would have give, so I don't know if he was telling it straight or not, but we took what we had on down the road and found that other place. There wasn't no line, so we did our business pretty fast. I was real satisfied with what we got. It was more money that I had ever seen in my life, and that man's uncle told me to bring as much as I could stand to bring, and he'd pay me the same rate for every bit of it.

"I took three more loads. Clothes, furniture, silverware, glasses, even paintings right off the wall. One of those paintings went for some big money. I don't know who was the painter. Might have been Michelangelo, I don't know. By the time we unloaded everything we didn't mean to keep, I had a big roll of bills in my pocket. I was a high roller.

"We took a little piece of it and went to gambling. Cards. Me playing stud poker, Harmon playing keno and bunco. I'd never heard of bunco in my life. I don't think he had either. I would lose a little at the poker table, Harmon would win a little back. Then we'd switch off a while. I thought we was coming out just about even, then Harmon put everything he had on one game and made out like gangbusters. We left Sabine Pass with enough money to burn a wet mule. As they say.

We saw Angel again before we left, and he asked had we been taken care of. We said we were very satisfied.

He said, which way y'all going, upriver or down?

I said, I wanted to see the ocean. I had lived all my life and never seen no ocean. I aimed to get a good look at it before I went anywhere.

Angel said, what you two fellas need to do is go down and see the ocean and just keep going. You go down to South America. Trinidad. That's where you need to go. Two men like yourselves can live a good life in Trinidad.

Well, that's what we did, pretty much. When I

saw that ocean, something inside me said, Art Patton, there ain't no going back. Ain't no going back now."

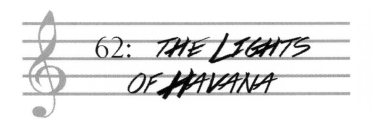

62: THE LIGHTS OF HAVANA

"That Lady Camargo took to the seas like a hog to husks. We pointed ourselves southeast and watched as the land behind us was swallowed up by water and more water. By the time the sun fell and the stars came out, it seemed like we were floating through space, like the stars had come right down to where we could almost touch them.

"It reminded me that old man in the sky I'd seen on the Conray plantation all those years ago. The old brown memory. Sitting out there on the bow of the boat, pushing our way through the rippling starlight before us, I think I realized who that old man was. Now, I've heard tell that when you look into the sky, you're looking into the past. I don't rightly remember where I heard that, but I wonder if whoever said such a thing had ever been out on a boat in the middle of the ocean. I'm telling you, out there, it seemed like that was all backward. Like maybe a whole bunch of things I'd spent my life thinking were all backward. Seemed more likely to me that you were gazing into the future. Where we haven't yet been. You hear me?

"If that were the case, it seemed to me that just maybe, I— way back when I was just plain Art, named like a dog and kept like one too— had been given some sort of gift. A short glimpse into my own destiny. Just a glimpse.

"Right there in that very moment, out there in that great big lake between the lights of home and the lights of Havana, under a whole mess of other lights that connected us all up, I looked back at myself, saw the truth and turned away. Away from myself, the Conray farm, Pattonia, and everything I had learned to think I knew.

"I told Harmon about it the next day, but it didn't seem as clear then. Like the starlight, it was still there, but it seemed farther away. We steamed on into the southeast, the wind picking up and pushing us right along. Sometimes a little rougher than we wanted it to, but, time to time we'd cut the engines and just let it ride. There were no hatchways to batten down, but, when it was necessary, we would board up the doorway to keep water from collecting.

"Soon enough, we could see the lights of Havana twinkling at us on the skyline.

"Those aren't stars, Harmon said.

"We cruised into port and tied up, spent the first night drinking rum and smoking cigars in a bar right on the beach. Liked that night so damn much, we spent the next fifty or sixty recreating it. The people were warm and the sun was friendly. In the afternoons, Harmon would pull out his guitar, and I would plunk around on the music stick, and, before we knew it, we had an audience. I could have stayed there the rest of my life real happy.

"It wasn't Angel's voice that made me pick up and move again. It was the Lady Camargo's. After all those years out of service, she wasn't ready to be moored so soon. Hell, maybe it was me who wasn't ready. I had spent my whole goddamn life within a ten mile radius. Could I help it if I wanted something different this time around?"

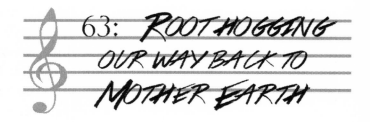

63: ROOT HOGGING OUR WAY BACK TO MOTHER EARTH

We could hear a distant chorus of coyotes chasing down a deer or something, and every now and then a possum or rabbit would scurry through the brush, but, other than that, it was the two of us and a big hole in the ground. We had a pretty good system going. Whenever one of us would hit a root that was too big to chop through with a shovel, the other one would grab the hand saw and start cutting. We might have been making fairly good time. I don't know. Truth is, we lost all track of time and could've been working through the night and right into the next day. Down at the bottom of that pit, it was hard to tell anything for sure.

I was working on a big pine root that cut right

through our path, and Ephriam stopped for a minute to rest his arms.

"Reckon this is what they mean when they talk about root hogging?" he said.

He went back to work. If you stopped for too long, your muscles would tighten up on you and you were screwed up for sure.

"Root hogging our way back to Mother Earth," I said.

I told him about my run-in with Billy Lee Conray the Third, and he said I was lucky I hadn't been killed and thrown in the well already. Ephriam had known the cousin of one of the boys Conray had shot in Nacalina. The colored one. I had assumed all three of them had been colored, but turned out that only one had.

"So what's the story?" I said.

"Which one you wanna hear?" he said.

"If there's a true one, I'll take that."

So it seems, Conray was living in Woden and working around the area doing some kind of pipelining or something. He hired these three boys to come along. It was right before Christmas, and he told them he could give them some Christmas money if they could help him finish up a couple of jobs before it got here.

They all met up at a store in Woden. Maybe the only store in Woden. He drove out into the middle of nowhere, pulled the car over on the side of the road, and told the colored boy to get out. Get out and run.

His two white friends looked at Conray like he was crazy.

The colored boy got out, and Conray chased along behind him in the car. Just close enough to keep him going, bumping right up against him when he got too tired. Finally, when he had enough of running him around, he pulled out a pistol and shot five bullets into the boy's back through the driver's side window. Of course, the other boys went hysterical.

"You so goddamn concerned about him, why don't you get the fuck out there and see if you can save him," Conray said.

One of the boys opened his car door and ran to check on his friend. Conray gassed the engine, toying with the kid. Then he reloaded his gun and shot him, just for being a nigger lover. The last boy was so scared, Conray had to pull him out of the back seat by an ear.

"I ain't gonna get your nigger loving blood all over my upholstery," he said.

I was enraged. How could a man get three years in prison for something like that. Even in Woden, Texas?

"Because it turned out not to be what really happened," said Ephriam. "That was the story Billy Conray told to people in Nacogdoches. At least a few people at some bar."

What Conray hadn't known was that one of the boys, a white kid with connections to an old money family in town, lived long enough to tell a pretty different version of things. Conray left all three kids for dead, and two of them were. But one of the white kids, a boy named Eddie Swain, was able to get to a nearby home. The couple there took him to a hospital in Lufkin.

Hospital staff brought in police, not even knowing that there were two more bodies left out in Nacalina. The police found everything out soon enough, and they also started finding evidence that raised more questions. What type of work were they supposed to be doing? Why did two of them have knives? Why was one hiding a chain inside of his coat? If they were working for Christmas money, why did the other white victim have two hundred dollars in his coat pocket?

Eddie Swain broke under the pressure and admitted that the three boys had attacked Conray and robbed him. They were attempting to take his car when he pulled a gun from beneath the driver's seat and started firing.

Swain died a few days later, and Conray wound up with ten years. Not for killing the colored boy, but for killing Eddie Swain, whose uncle was a trial lawyer.

Some people will lie about just about anything, and you can never be perfectly sure of another man's motivations.

64: BLIND LEMON JEFFERSON AND PAPA LEGBA

"Harmon's eyes were starting to look yellow. He never looked back, so it wasn't homesickness. It wasn't seasickness. It was just plain old sickness. And we were back on the water, no land in sight. Most days, he would spend inside the bunk, flat on his back and rocked to sleep by the rise and fall of the waves. Most nights, on the bow of the boat, watching the stars like he was waiting for a sign. I don't know what he was thinking, and I didn't ask.

"When we reached Haiti, we went into a village just outside of Port-au-Prince and found a bocar, a voodoo chief. They called him a leaf doctor because he used plants and natural medicines. And he played a drum which made Harmon very happy.

"Any doctor who plays a drum on the job is using my kind of medicine, he said.

"Harmon spent part of an afternoon, deep into a night in the care of the bocar, and he immediately felt better. We even spent the following evening playing music with the doctor and several of his friends. Harmon sang Blind lemon Jefferson songs while the bocar and a man named Jean Telly played drums and called on Papa Legba and Lasirèn to give us safe passage as we continued on our way.

"That Papa Legba seemed like a spirit I could get along with. He seemed familiar to me. I got the Jean Telly to paint his picture on the back of the music stick, and he painted an old man with a hat.

"That looks like me, I said. You painted me.

"Harmon did good for the next week. He stayed in his bunk a good portion of the time, but he spent most of that time reading. He loved to read, and when he had a book in his hand, I knew two things. One was that he was happy. Because books made him happy. From Mark Twain to Edgar Rice Burroughs to James Weldon Johnson, he often had a new one in one hand even as he was closing up the old one. The other thing I knew— or at least thought I knew— was that when he was reading, he thought he was going to live, at least long enough to finish the book.

"That's why I was startled to wake up one morning not far from the coast of Trinidad and find my friend Harmon Littlejohn, sometimes better remembered as Little John Harmon, dead in his bunk with an unfinished copy of Canterbury Tales in his hand.

"I had felt alone before, but I'm not sure I ever knew what lonesome meant until then. The next couple of days were longer than they had any right to be, and full of much thought. Funny enough, it reminded me of when George Delafield died. How I had promised to see to it that he was put safely into Mount Violet, close to those he loved.

"Harmon had told me, back before we reached Haiti, that if he were to die on the Lady Camargo, he wanted to be buried at sea, like King Arthur.

"King Arthur wasn't buried in no sea, I said.

"Harmon said he was too.

"King Arthur ain't even for real, I said. He's ain't nothing but a made up story.

"Harmon was hard headed if he was anything, and he was having none of it.

"I thought about it for a long time, but I never could bring myself to dropping Harmon off in the ocean, like he was a worm for the fishes. I wrapped him up good and tight and sailed on for South America. When I reached the shores of Trinidad— and let me tell you, they were a beautiful sight to see; it was like looking at goddamn paradise after you just sailed through a hurricane of blues— I knew this was the place to let Harmon find his rest. We had made it."

\

65: THE REAL TRUE ART

The water table is fairly shallow around the Patton's Landing area, mostly because of the river. There are springs that feed into it, and the ground in general in fairly moist, as long as you stay within sight of the river. We were probably eight or ten feet down and getting close to the bottom. You could tell because you could see a water line which told you that there had actually been water in the bottom of it fairly recently, probably when the river flooded during the spring.

Ephriam was telling Art stories, and I was imagining all the things we could possibly find once we reached the bottom. The bones of the first Art. The real, true Art. This poor baby who had had a lifetime of being Art snatched from him.

There could be coins. Old confederate coins. Worthless now except to collectors. Thrown into the well for the amusement and good luck of people whose fortune had run out long ago. Maybe family heirlooms hidden during the war. Gold and silver. A gun thrown away to destroy evidence.

All of these things and more were circling around in my head. To the point I didn't pay much mind when Ephriam mentioned that the stone walls were getting soft and crumbly. We had a rope ladder tied off at a tree trunk at the top, with two-by-fours set about every three feet or so. He had used it to climb up into a barn on the Whitaker property. Ephriam must have either sensed some kind of trouble or had a moment of panic or claustrophobia, because he reached up and pulled on the rope, stepped on the first step like he wanted to practice, just in case it was needed. He took one step and then dropped back down, seeming satisfied. I remember his clapping his hands together and smiling at me. He was just about to say something when it began to rain dirt. Just a little at first, like when a summer rain comes across the river. And then it kept on coming.

We both looked up and, at first, I thought the west wall of the well was coming down. Then I understood what had happened. The dirt we had been shifting out of the well, stacking up on that side, was coming back at us.

"We've gotta get out of here," I said.

CONSTELLATIONS

I pushed Ephriam up the ladder, knowing that if he didn't make it out alive, I would never be able to face up to Oda Whitaker. I've heard people say that when something big and bad hits them, everything seems to run in slow motion. Far as I can tell, I would tend to say that's utter bullshit. Everything happened so fast, I didn't know what hit me. In hindsight, I know that it was a big wall of dirt. Within seconds, I was swallowed up whole like the man in the Bible.

I don't know how to describe to you what it feels like to be buried alive. It's like drowning, except you're drowning in dirt. I opened my mouth to scream and got a mouthful of it. I opened my eyes and saw nothing but it. I tried to claw at it, and my hands wouldn't move. I felt like I was going under. I couldn't breathe.

I had no idea where Ephriam was. If he had made it out or was buried above me. I could hear nothing but the pounding of my own heart, the blood rushing through my head, my muffled attempts to suck air into my lungs, which seemed to be on fire.

I remember shutting down. Letting go. Becoming the blackness that surrounded me. The very last memory I had was that I was already buried so no one would have to go to any trouble.

66: SAFRANA'S STORIES

There is no such thing as the story of someone's life.

1. Each life is made up of thousands and thousands of stories, all going on at different times, overlapping each other, ending and then starting over again.

2. Our stories all overlap with each other's too. Harmon's stories overlap with mine, and mine overlap with somebody else. Lots of somebody elses.

3. Our stories are affected by and overlapped by stories that came before us. Ancestors and people we may or may not even know by name. And we are affecting the stories of people who are not yet born.

I lived in Trinidad for three years, mostly in the

suburbs of Port of Spain. I made friends, and I made money, mostly playing music— and sometimes cards— in Saint James. I met a lady named Safrana there, and we became quite close. I had my own house there, close to Cocorite on the Western Main Road. A nice house with a screened in front porch where the neighbors would come and spend evenings.

Safrana worked in a home for young girls. It was in a good part of the town. A good job, because her sisters worked on a sugarcane plantation. They were paid for their work, but the hours and conditions were terrible. It reminded me of the Conray plantation. I told Safrana she could come and live with me, but her father would have never allowed it. To make things more difficult, Safrana was involved in a group fighting for workers' rights. Trying to reform things, make for a better life.

I also met a man from Ghana in Saint James, and convinced me that I should go to Africa. He said every man of color needs to go at least one time and have a look around. I kept that in mind for a while. Sometimes I wouldn't see the man from Ghana for a while, and then, when we would run into each other, he would say, I thought you must have gone to Africa.

Finally, one night, Safrana and I had an argument, and she said she wouldn't be coming around for a while. I took it as a sign and packed up my belongings. Left my yellow house on Western Main and shoved off from Port of Spain early the following morning.

Sometimes I still miss that house. Sometimes I miss the smell of fish and chicken barbecuing in the neighboring houses. The Lambie souse. The Calypso. The Carnival. And sometimes I wonder whatever happened to Safrana and her sisters. What are Safrana's stories, and does she remember when one of hers crossed mine.

67: BAPTIZED BY DIRT

I was down there with the bones of the true Art and Blue Dick and the hidden silver and God knows what. Dead as a rock in the weary land. My wellspring had dried up. I don't know how long I was there. I had no dream or vision about entering through the narrow gates of heaven or busting hell open wide either. I didn't hear angels call my name.

At some point, I did hear voices. Faint voices. And I saw a light too, but it was weak.

"Get that lamp down here closer. I think I see him."

I didn't make any attempt to say or do anything. I was picking up signals but all transmissions were down. A few moments later, I could feel the ground open up and then a hand wrapped around mine. I squeezed, and my senses flooded back into me, but they were confounded and out of sorts, as if they'd all come back topsy-turvy. Out of order and in the wrong places.

"Be careful."

I recognized the voice, but, in my confusion, I thought I was Art Patton and the voice was Harmon Littlejohn. I turned my face to the light.

"Harm."

I could feel nothing below my chest. As far as I knew, that's all there was left of me.

"I think he said something. Grab this arm and pull. Don't yank, just pull."

Moments later, I was pulled free of the grave and rolled onto the ground. My nose, my mouth, my lungs all full of dirt. Baptized in it and born again. I saw a face that I knew. It wasn't Harmon. It wasn't Ephriam.

He bent down next to me and put a canteen to my lips.

"Take just a little bit."

The water was cold, and I could feel it going all the way down. Like I was parched ground and it was the first rain in too long. My faculties somewhat restored, I wondered where Ephriam was. Had I seen him. Was he still in the well. Had he been pulled out too. Was he alive.

I looked back at the man with the canteen. Billy Lee Conray the Third.

"I'm gonna tell you this one time. I'm gonna help you get your friend up to the road. Then you're gonna take him and scram. You're gonna tear ass out of here for good, understand. Because if I catch either one of you out here again, you can bet your balls, it's gonna be real bad news."

Ephriam wanted to take me back to Oda, but I knew I had to get home. I'm not sure how he made it from there. I suspect Paul took him. What the two of them might have said, I have no idea. I do know Paul covered for me when questions were raised the next day. I hurt for a week or two after, and I had a limp for about as long, but that was about it for physical aftershocks. The mental ones proved tougher to deal with. Sometimes I still wake up in the night fighting my way out of that damn well. Sometimes Art is pulling me to safety. Sometimes it's Billy Conray. Most of the time, there's nobody there at all. Just me, the dirt and the darkness.

68: *MAA NGI TUDD ART PATTON*

"Africa.

"The west coast of Africa, the nation of Senegal specifically, became an extremely important part of my story, even if I choose not to tell all of it. The truth is, we only know pieces of another person's story. The pieces they tell. Or the pieces that overlap with ours.

"Parts of my story I keep to myself. Everybody does.

I arrived in Dakar toward the end of 1928, right in the middle of a walkout by seamen there in the port. I might have taken a job there, but I couldn't speak French or Wolof. I was a new face in town. A negro, but an American. I met a Frenchman who could speak English, and word quickly got around that I had been living in Trinidad and had connections to some of the union organizers there. Within a week, I was helping to put together underground meetings with people there in Dakar.

I never cared for politics. I had only found myself in their surroundings by happenstance. By mistake really. Soon enough, I was able to get away from the port area. I went up the coast to Ndar, settling a couple of miles up the Senegal River. There, much to my surprise, I would spend the next twenty-four years. Ndar reminded me of Havana, both to the eye and to the ear. I was happy to discover that Cuban music was popular on the radio and in the streets. I played more music than I had since Harmon and me had played in Havana and Haiti.

I learned Wolof. After a year or two, it seems the only time I used my native tongue was when I was reading. I would go years without hearing it spoken. Even my thoughts and dreams began coming to me in Wolof.

"Maa ngi tudd Art Patton. Ameriik laa joge. Dégg nga?

I converted the Lady Camargo into a fishing boat and made a decent living, but fortune found me even on the Senegal River. Four years after I arrived, I met a man named Sadio who was getting into the peanut farming business. I invested with him and made many more dollars from that venture than I ever did fishing.

Sadio was also responsible, indirectly, for another

momentous occurrence. As time went on, I would take trips down to Dakar three or four times a year. Sadio would show me the latest developments with the business, and he would pay me my portion of the profits. I would then buy supplies and anything I needed for the boat and enjoy a night of entertainment. This would include music and a meal and, as time went by, a visit to one of the working girls close to the port. A cagga.

There was one particular cagga named Marietou who I would call on with some regularity. She liked to hear stories from back home in Texas, and I began to enjoy telling them almost as much as being with her. I had been with her four or five times, and then, one night I came to her room and she was gone. It reminded me of Safrana on Western Main Road in Port of Spain, Trinidad, but I had learned my lesson this time. I had grown wiser, or at least more strong-headed. I went looking for her.

I spent a day and a half longer in the city, following directions from people who thought they might know her. I finally found her in the home of an old lady who thought I was her pimp. It took some doing, but I managed to get her to let me see her.

"Fukki minit."

Ten minutes.

In the next ten minutes, my life would change once again.

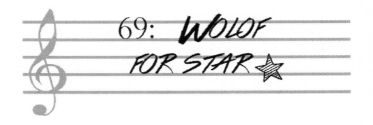

69: **WOLOF FOR STAR** ★

My daughter was born to Marietou Mbengue on January 20, 1938. I named her Jo Biidéo. Jo for Jodora. Biidéo, Wolof for star. I was able to get Marietou a job working for Sadio, and she raised Jo Biidéo until she was of school age. There were no schools for girls in her location, so I paid a woman who worked in a Catholic private school to teach her. During that time, she would live with her mother during school terms and stay with me when it was out. I would play music for her and tell her stories of my days in Pattonia, my life as Art and only Art, of mean old Blue Dick, of Harmon Littlejohn.

Sometimes the stories seemed unreal to me. At night, I could go out on the bow of the boat, look upriver and almost make myself believe I was back on the Angelina. Ndar was home, and yet Pattonia continued to pull at me like a mischievous child. I would look up at the moon and think about the people looking at it from back there. Angelina, river of angels. Angel in Sabine Pass. I had been guided by them. Did the people standing on the banks of that dirty little river understand. Did they believe that it could take them to the other side of the world. To another life.

I had been totally and completely transfigured. It took me a while to understand. Understand may be the wrong word. I'm not sure I will ever understand it. But I learned to believe it. I had first heard the word from the bocar, or maybe it was Jean Telly, in Haiti. They saw something happening that set me apart. More lives. More stories.

Jean Telly said that Jesus himself had been transfigured.

As Jo Biidéo grew, she started to tell stories of her own. Her stories all looked ahead instead of back. She talked of where she wanted to go, the things she wanted to see. I began to see things through her eyes. I began to understand that I had put the Lady Camargo back together not for myself. Not to get myself to Haiti or Trinidad or even to Senegal. I had rebuilt it to take Jo Biidéo on her journey. We began to talk about coming to America.

In 1956, she would arrive in Charleston with me, and by the end of that year, she would be enrolled in

Stillman College in Tuscaloosa, Alabama. Jo Biidéo Patton of Dakar, Senegal. Who never would have had a story to tell if not for Marietou. If not for a nameless Ghanaian in Saint James. If not for the Haitian bocar. Angel in Sabine Pass. Harmon Littlejohn in Pattonia. George Delafield.

It all comes back to George Delafield. I can't say he ever had any idea what his gift to me would turn into. But I also can't say he would be surprised. He told me once, many years ago, while we were sitting in front of the seed store playing bones, that one of us was bound to live forever. Maybe he just meant that either of us would do anything we could to outlive the other. Or maybe he knew more than he was letting on.

Anything I did that was truly special was done there at that damn seed store. That's where I got it in my hard head that I didn't want to die there. You keep yourself from dying long enough, you're bound to go a few places. Bound to collect a few stories. Bound to learn how to make some kind of a racket that's never been made before.

You'll get yourself into all kinds of things you never expected. You might even get yourself transfigured.

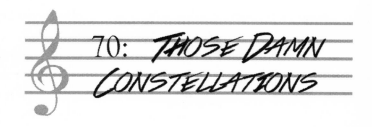

70: THOSE DAMN CONSTELLATIONS

I watched for Art at The Pepper Pot and all up and down Patton's Landing Road, but I never did see or hear anything from him. Ephriam and me wondered if he had gone back to Alabama to see his daughter, but neither of us had any way of pursuing the matter. I wrote a short article for the Gazette about his appearance at the juke joint. I don't think anyone ever read it but me. I messed around with the idea of writing something more substantial, but I decided I couldn't tell part of the story unless I told all of it.

Sometimes I would drive out to the river, away from the street lights in town, where the stars seemed to multiply. I would find the Big Dipper and the

North Star and wonder if, just maybe, Art was looking at it as well.

I never will forget what he said about constellations. Art, who looked up into the sky and saw strange signs as a small boy, who followed those same signs halfway around the world and back again, knew his way around the sky too.

"The same constellations that brought Columbus over here, that brought all kinds of explorers to the new world, well, those are the same goddamn constellations that took enslaved negroes to freedom up in the north. The stars don't care who reads them. Don't give a damn. Don't care if you got black skin or white skin or no skin at all. See, the constellations don't even give a damn whether you're a good man or a bad man. You can be running away from evil or running smack dab into its arms. Don't make them no difference.

"This whole world is sailing through the sky. Going around and around, never staying in one place. You can sit right here on the banks of the Angelina River and think you're never going anywhere, and, in one way of seeing it, you couldn't be more wrong.

But here's the thing I'm trying to tell you. Nothing stays the same. Time keeps moving, and we keep moving with it. What's here today will be gone tomorrow. But no matter what else happens. No matter how many days and years and lifetimes go by. No matter how far we sail through the sky, when you look up, those damn constellations are gonna be there. They don't ever change. You may not be able to count the stars, but you can sure enough count on that."

That might be my favorite thing the man ever said, and he wasn't on a stage when he said it. He was standing in the dark and looking me straight in the eye. Art Conray Patton was a slave. He was a son and a brother. He was a carpenter. A friend. A boat captain. A musician. He might have been transfigured. But more than all these things, he was following the stars. He was an explorer.

71: *RIVERBOAT WRECKAGE*

Almost a week after the Gazette ran my article, a white man came walking into the Gazette office and asked for me. He was a history professor at the college in Nacogdoches, and he had somehow picked up a copy of my story. He didn't have the regulation Army haircut. He looked young to be a professor.

"You the one who wrote the review on Art Patton?"

I had been writing an article on upcoming family reunions. I stood up and shook the man's hand. Dr. Coleman.

"Yes sir," I said.

He seemed nervous. Most likely because he felt out of place.

"This Pepper Pot," he said. "It's over on the road to Marion's Ferry?"

I said that it was.

"Do the whites go there? What I mean to say, are they welcomed?"

I thought it funny the way he said they, as if he weren't one. I told him that I had seen a white person or two there, usually saw mill employees from around Kelty's, usually with colored co-workers. We wound up talking about Mance Lipscomb, who he had just seen at a picnic in Navasota, Texas. I had never seen Mance, but I knew who he was. I took down the man's phone number and agreed to call him up the next time I was headed to The Pepper Pot.

Almost as a second thought, he reached inside his jacket and handed me a page from a newspaper.

"I thought you might be interested in this."

I glanced at it. The Beaumont Enterprise. Dr. Coleman excused himself, saying he hoped to hear from me again soon. I returned to my desk, pushing the family reunion news aside and unfolding the article in my hands.

It was dated September 24, 1957.

"This week, a local hunter and his son discovered the wrecked remains of a steamboat just south of the Sabine Pass area in an area hit hard by Hurricane Audrey. The steamboat had been hidden by years of forest growth and changes in the river brought about by newer, man-made lakes. The boat, with its name Lady Camargo worn but still legible on the side, had likely been used to bring loads of cotton down the Neches River, possibly as long as one hundred years ago.

There were no human remains or signs of the boats crew."

I shared the article with Ephriam that same evening. I had to share it with someone. It was too much to take home and file away. I drove out to Oda's place, only to find that he had moved into town. It was late by the time I found his address and knocked at his door. We talked on his front porch. Short and straight to the point. For reasons I wasn't up to discussing, I felt low. Low and lonesome and let down.

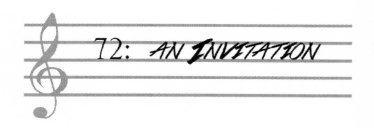

72: AN INVITATION

Sometime in the spring of the following year, I took a trip to The Pepper Pot with my friend Bob Coleman. Juke Boy Bonner was playing. I had heard a couple of his records and liked them. When we arrived, Jay Henry was working the bar, and there was already a decent crowd in the place. Juke Boy was setting up in the opposite corner from where Art had played, a wise decision I thought.

I walked up to the bar to order two beers. Jay Henry did the pouring and then told me to hold on for just a minute He disappeared under the bar and came up with a cigar box full of papers. He rustled around in it and fished out an envelope with my name on it.

"I believe this is for you, young man. It's been setting out here a while."

I turned the envelope over in my hand. Aside from my name, no other clues. I took it and the two cups and returned to our table. Juke Boy was tuning his guitar, a pretty white Fender with a red pick guard. He had a harmonica rack that made it look like he was wearing some kind of neck brace. The first one I had ever seen.

The envelope contained a card and a piece of paper. On the card was printed:

Stillman College
announces the Commencement Exercises

Saturday, May 16

Nineteen Hundred Fifty-Nine

Tuscaloosa, Alabama

and then beneath that:

Jo Biidéo Patton

A piece of paper accompanied it, with the scratched message: *Do you think you can find room for this somewhere in your newspaper?*

73: ABOUT THAT ACETATE

A month later, I was standing in the office of Maydell Records on Hadley Street in Houston. I had two copies of the acetate for "This Little Light Of Mine" under my arm and a fresh rejection from the Peacock label, who said it was an old-timey song that nobody wanted to hear again. Marcell Ashbrook at Maydell took one look at what I had and hurried me into his office.

"This is the same Art Patton who played in Africa? The same Art Patton who played on WERD out of Atlanta? The one who played with the 5 Royales at the Saenger in New Orleans?"

I looked at the photographs on Mister Ashbrook's wall and tried to find someone I recognized.

"I think he's probably most of those same ones," I said.

There was a photograph of Mister Ashbrook with Mahalia Jackson and another man, and a different one of him and The Soul Stirrers, his arm around Sam Cooke like they were old friends. I signed the papers, and he agreed to release the single before even hearing it. They called it "This Blues Light Of Mine (Part One)" by Art Patton featuring Eulalie Glover. The flip side had part two and it was even better.

Marcell Ashbrook said Art had established quite a name playing in Africa and had recorded a handful of songs for a small label over there.

"Radio songs, with a dude named Cachao," he said. "They play his shit on the radio from Dakar to Nigeria and up to France. Cuba too. Impossible to find in America. Impossible."

Art had been making waves as he made his way across the south, picking up dates on the circuit and building word of mouth along the way. So much that Marcell had been put on notice by a label head in New Orleans.

"He's from your neck of the woods. Look out for him."

As far as I know, the Maydell single is the only recording he ever made in the United States. Mister Ashbrook got in touch with me a couple of times over the next year or so, asking if I had heard more from Art. Then the phone stopped ringing.

The record never sold in any great numbers, never became a hot collector's item, although I've heard that copies turn up every now and then. In old boxes, at garage sales, places where people don't have any idea who he is or what he did or even what they have in their hands.

I was talking to a music collector not too long ago, and Art's name came up. She wanted to know if I still had a copy of the record. I played it for her twice. She sat there for a minute after the needle lifted up. Then she leaned in.

"So what do you think the real story is?"

I think the real story is this. I think Art Patton and Harmon Littlejohn left Pattonia in 1924 headed for Sabine Pass. I think they made it that far and sold all of George Delafield's possessions. I think they either decided to ditch the Lady Camargo or ran into trouble between there and the gulf. I think they bought a ticket on a boat bound for Cuba. I think they went from there to Haiti. I think somewhere between Haiti and Trinidad, Art Conray Patton got sick and died. And I think somewhere between Trinidad and Senegal, Harmon Littlejohn— who had been known to change his name to Little John Harmon if he thought it would help him be remembered— was transfigured. I think he absorbed everything he had known about the man who was born into slavery, who had been given the name of a dead brother himself. And I think he took the story, added it to his own and pushed it further up and further in, as C.S. Lewis said.

I didn't tell this music collector that, of course. You choose which stories you tell and which ones you keep to yourself.

TIM BRYANT

ABOUT THE AUTHOR

Tim's first novel DUTCH CURRIDGE was published in 2010. He has since published two more in the Dutch Curridge Series, including 2014's SPIRIT TRAP, for which he was named one of the Top Five Texas Authors of the year by BookPeople in Austin. His short story "Doll's Eyes" was published in Subterranean Press' IMPOSSIBLE MONSTERS. He lives in East Texas with his wife and two children.

92602995R00167

Made in the USA
Columbia, SC
02 April 2018